EXOTIC PLEASURES

Peter Carey grew up in Bacchus Marsh, Victoria and now lives in Sydney. His first, best-selling book, *The Fat Man in History*, was followed by *War Crimes*, which won him the New South Wales Premier's Award in 1980. His novel *Bliss* won the same award in 1982 as well as the Miles Franklin and National Book Council awards. The film *Bliss*, based on the novel, won three Australian Film Institute awards in 1985, including best feature film. His novel *Illywhacker* (1985) won the Victorian Premier's Award, the *Age* Book of the Year Award, the NBC Award for Australian Literature, the FAW Barbara Ramsden Award, and was shortlisted for the Booker Prize. *Oscar and Lucinda*, Peter Carey's best-selling novel, won the 1988 Booker Prize, the Talking Book of the Year Award, the 1989 Miles Franklin and National Book Council award, the Foundation for Australian Literary Studies award, and the 1990 Adelaide Festival Award for Literature.

PETER CAREY

EXOTIC PLEASURES

University of Queensland Press

First published 1980 by Faber and Faber Ltd
Published 1990 by University of Queensland Press
Box 42, St Lucia, Queensland 4067 Australia

These stories were first published in *The Fat Man in History* (UQP 1974) and
War Crimes (UQP 1979)

Printed in Australia by The Book Printer, Maryborough

Creative writing program assisted by
the Literature Board of the Australia
Council, the Federal Government's
arts funding and advisory body

Cataloguing in Publication Data
National Library of Australia

Carey, Peter 1943- .
  Exotic pleasures.

  I. Title.

A823.3

ISBN 0 7022 2322 0

Contents

The Fat Man in History

1

His feet are sore. The emporium seems endless as he shuffles an odd-legged shuffle with the double-bed sheets under his arm. It is like a nightmare—the exit door in sight but not coming any closer, the oppressive heat, the constant swarm of bodies flowing towards him like insects drawn towards, then repelled by, a speeding vehicle.

He is sweating badly, attempting to look calm. The sheets are badly wrapped. He wrapped them himself, surprising himself with his own nerve. He took the sheets (double, because there were no singles in blue) and walked to the wrapping counter where he pulled out a length of brown paper and set to work. To an assistant looking at him queryingly he said, smiling meekly, "You don't object?" The assistant looked away.

His trousers are large, floppy, and old-fashioned. Fortunately they have very large pockets and the pockets now contain several tins of smoked oysters. The smoked oysters are easy, always in big tubs outside the entrance to the self-service section. He has often wondered why they do this, why put them outside? Is it to make them easier to steal, because they are difficult to sell? Is it their way of providing for him and his friends? Is there possibly a fat man who has retained his position in the emporium? He enjoys himself with these theories, he has a love of such constructions, building ideas like card-houses, extending them until he gets dizzy and trembles at their heights.

Approaching the revolving door he hesitates, trying to judge the best way to enter the thing. The door is turning fast, spewing people into the store, last-minute shoppers. He chooses his space and moves forward, bustling to get there in time. Deidre, as tiny and bird-like as she always was, is thrown out of the revolving door, collides with him, hisses "slob" at him, and scurries into the store, leaving him with a sense of dull amazement, surprise that such a pretty face could express such fear and hatred so quickly.

Of course it wasn't Deidre. But Alexander Finch reflects that it could have been. As he sadly circles inside the revolving door and walks slowly along the street he thinks how strange it is that the revolution should have produced this one idea that would affect his life so drastically: to be fat is to be an oppressor, to be greedy, to be pre-revolutionary. It is impossible to say if it arose from the people or was fed to them by the propaganda of the revolution. Certainly in the years before the revolution most fat men were either Americans, stooges for the Americans, or wealthy supporters of the Americans. But in those years the people were of a more reasonable mind and could accept the idea of fat men like Alexander Finch being against the Americans and against the old Danko regime.

Alexander Finch had always thought of himself as possessing a lovable face and figure. He had not thought this from any conceit. At school they had called him "Cuddles", and on the paper everyone called him "Teddy" or "Teddy Bear". He had signed his cartoons "Teddy" and when he included himself in a cartoon he was always a bewildered, rotund man with a large bum, looking on the antics of the world with smiling, fatherly eyes.

But somehow, slowly, the way in which the world looked at Alexander Finch and, in consequence, the way Alexander Finch looked at himself, altered. He was forced to become a different cartoon, one of his own "Fat Americans": grotesque, greedy, an enemy of the people.

But in the early days after the revolution the change had not taken place. Or, if it had, Finch was too busy to notice it. As secretary of the Thirty-second District he took notes, recorded minutes, wrote weekly bulletins, drafted the ten-day reports to the Central Committee of Seventy-five, and still, somehow, found time to do a cartoon for his paper every day and to remember that General Kooper was spelt with a "K" and not a "C" (Miles Cooper being one of the infamous traitors of the revolution). In addition he was responsible for inspecting and reporting on the state of properties in the Thirty-second District and investigating cases of hardship and poverty wherever he found them. And if, during these early days, he occasionally became involved in unpleasant misunderstandings he regarded them as simply that, nothing more. People were accustomed to regarding all fat officials as either American or Danko men, because only the Americans and their friends had had enough food to become fat on. Occasionally Finch attempted to explain the nature of glandular fat and to point out that he wasn't a real official but rather the cartoonist "Teddy" who had always been anti-Danko.

Finch was occasionally embarrassed by his fatness in the early days when the people were hungry. But, paradoxically, it wasn't until the situation improved, when production had reached and passed the pre-revolutionary figure and when the distribution problems had finally been more or less ironed out, that the fat question came to the fore. And then, of course, food was no problem at all. If anything there was a surfeit and there was talk of dumping grain on the world market. Instead it was dumped in the sea.

Even then the district committees and the Committee of Seventy-five never passed any motions directly relating to fat men. Rather the word "fat" entered slyly into the language as a new adjective, as a synonym for greedy, ugly, sleazy, lazy, obscene, evil, dirty, dishonest, untrustworthy. It was unfair. It was not a good time to be a fat man.

Alexander Finch, now secretary of the clandestine "Fat Men Against The Revolution", carries his stolen double-bed sheets and his cans of smoked oysters northwards through the hot city streets. His narrow slanting eyes are almost shut and he looks out at the world through a comforting curtain of eyelashes. He moves slowly, a fat man with a white cotton shirt, baggy grey trousers, and a slight limp that could be interpreted as a waddle. His shirt shows large areas of sweat, like daubs, markings deliberately applied. No one bumps him. At the traffic lights he stands to one side, away from the crowds. It seems to be a mutual arrangement.

The sheets under his arm feel heavy and soggy. He is not sure that he has gotten away with it. They may be following him still (he dares not look around), following him to the house, to discover what else he may have stolen. He smiles at the thought of all those empty cans of smoked oysters in the incinerator in the back yard, all those hundreds of cans they will find. And the beer keg Fantoni stole. And the little buddha he stole for Fantoni's birthday but somehow kept for himself, he felt so sorry for (or was it fond of?) the little fat statue. He accuses himself of self-love but reflects that a little self-love is tonic for a fat man in these times.

Two youths run past him, bumping him from either side. He assumes it was intentional but is uncertain. His whole situation is like that, a tyranny of subtlety. To be fired from his job with the only newspaper that had been continually sympathetic to Kooper and his ideas for "slovenliness" and "bad spelling". He had laughed out loud. "Bad spelling." It was almost a tradition that cartoonists were bad spellers. It was expected of them and his work was always checked carefully for literals. But now they said his spelling was a nuisance and wasteful of time, and anyway he was "generally slovenly in dress and attitude". Did "slovenly" really mean "fat"? He didn't ask them. He didn't wish to embarrass them.

2

Milligan's taxi is parked in front of the house. The taxi is like Milligan: it is very bright and shiny and painted in stripes of iridescent blue and yellow. Milligan spray-painted it himself. It looks like a dodgem car from Luna Park, right down to the random collection of pink stars stencilled on the driver's door.

Milligan is probably asleep.

Behind Milligan's taxi the house is very still and very drab, painted in the colours of railway stations and schools: hard green and dirty cream. Rust shows through the cream paint on the cast-iron balcony and two pairs of large baggy underpants hang limply from a line on the upstairs verandah.

It is one of six such houses, all identical, surrounded by high blocks of concrete flats and areas of flat waste land where dry thistles grow. The road itself is a major one and still retains some of its pre-revolutionary grandeur: rows of large elms form an avenue leading into the city.

The small front garden is full of weeds and Glino's radishes. Finch opens the front door cautiously, hoping it will be cooler inside but knowing that it won't be. In the half-dark he gropes around on the floor, feeling for letters. There are none—Fantoni must have taken them. He can still make out the dark blotches on the door where May sat and banged his head for three hours. No one has bothered to remove the blood.

Finch stands in the dark passage and listens. The house has the feeling of a place where no one works, a sort of listlessness. May is upstairs playing his Sibelius record. It is very scratched and it makes May morose, but it is the only record he has and he plays it incessantly. The music filters through the heavy heat of the passage and Finch hopes that Fantoni is not in the kitchen reading his "correspondence"—he doesn't wish Fantoni to see the sheets. He shuffles slowly down the passage, past the foot of the high, steep stairs, through the strange little cupboard where Glino cooks his vegetarian meals in two battered aluminium saucepans, and enters the kitchen where Fantoni, wearing a florid Hawaiian shirt and smoking a cigar, is reading his "correspondence" and tugging at the large moustache which partially obscures his small mouth. Finch has often thought it strange that such a large man should have such a small mouth. Fantoni's hands are also small but his forearms are large and muscular. His head is almost clean shaven, having the shortest of bristles covering it, and the back of his head is divided by a number of strange creases. Fantoni is the youngest of the six fat men who live in the house. An ex-parking officer, aged about twenty-eight, he is the most accomplished thief of them all. Without Fantoni they would all come close to starving, eking out a living on their pensions. Only Milligan has any other income.

Fantoni has connections everywhere. He can arrange food. He can arrange anything. He can arrange anything but the dynamite he needs to blow up the 16 October Statue. He has spent two months looking for the dynamite. Fantoni is the leader and driving force of the "Fat Men Against The Revolution". The others are like a hired army, fighting for Fantoni's cause which is to "teach the little monkeys a lesson".

Fantoni does not look up as Finch enters. He does not look

up when Finch greets him. He does nothing to acknowledge Finch's presence. Because he is occupied with "my correspondence", the nature of which he has never revealed to anyone. Finch, for once, is happy that Fantoni doesn't look up, and continues out on to the porch with the green fibreglass sunroof, past Fantoni's brand new bicycle and Glino's herbs, along the concrete path, past the kitchen window, and comes to what is known as "the new extensions".

"The new extensions" are two bedrooms that have been added on to the back of the house. Their outside walls are made from corrugated iron, painted a dark, rusty red. Inside they are a little more pleasant. One is empty. Finch has the other. Finch's room is full of little pieces of bric-a-brac—books, papers, his buddha, a Rubens print, postcards from Italy with reproductions of Renaissance paintings. He has an early map of Iceland on the wall above the plywood bedhead, a grey goatskin rug covering the biggest holes in the maroon felt carpet, a Chinese paper lantern over the naked light globe.

He opens the door, steps back a pace, and pulls a huge comic fatman's face to register his disgust to some invisible observer.

The room has no insulation. And with each day of heat it has become hotter and hotter. At 4 a.m. it becomes a little cooler and at 7 a.m. it begins to heat up again. The heat brings out the strange smells of previous inhabitants, strange sweats and hopes come oozing out in the heat, ghosts of dreams and spilt Pine-o-Cleen.

The window does not open. There is no fly-wire screen on the door. He can choose between suffocation and mosquitoes.

Only a year ago he did a series of cartoons about housing conditions. He had shown corrugated iron shacks, huge flies, fierce rats, and Danko himself pocketing the rent. Danko's men had called on him after the fourth one had appeared. They threatened to jail him for treason, to beat him up, to torture him. He was very frightened, but they did nothing.

And now he is living in a corrugated iron room with huge blow-flies and the occasional rat. In a strange way it pleases him that he is no longer an observer, but it is a very small pleasure, too small to overcome the sense of despair that the smells and the suffocating heat induce in him.

He opens the roughly wrapped parcel of sheets and arranges

them on the bed. The blue is cool. That is why he wanted the blue so badly because it is cooler than white, and because it doesn't show the dirt so badly. The old sheets have turned a disgusting brown. If they were not listed in the inventory he would take them out and burn them. Instead he rolls them up and stuffs them under the bed.

If Fantoni had seen the sheets there would have been a row. He would have been accused, again, of self-indulgence, of stealing luxuries instead of food. But Fantoni can always arrange sufficient food.

He peels off the clinging, sweat-soaked clothes and throws them on the goatskin rug. Bending over to remove his socks he catches sight of his body. He stands slowly, in amazement. He is Alexander Finch whose father was called Senti but who called himself Finch because he sold American cigarettes on the black market and thought the name Finch very American. He is Alexander Finch, thirty-five years old, very fat, very tired, and suddenly, hopelessly sad. He has four large rolls of fat descending like a flesh curtain suspended from his navel. His spare tyres. He holds the fat in his hand, clenching it, wishing to tear it away. He clenches it until it hurts, and then clenches harder. For all the Rubens prints, for all the little buddhas, he is no longer proud or even happy to be fat. He is no longer Teddy. But he is not yet Fantoni or Glino—he doesn't hate the little monkeys. And, as much as he might pretend to, he is never completely convincing. They suspect him of mildness.

He is Finch whose father was called Senti, whose father was not fat, whose mother was not fat, whose grandfather may well have been called Chong or Ching—how else to explain the narrow eyes and the springy black hair?

3

There are six fat men in the house: Finch, Fantoni, May, Milligan, Glino, and one man who has never divulged his name. The-man-who-won't-give-his-name has been here from the beginning. He is taller, heavier, and stronger than any of the others, Fantoni included. Finch has estimated his weight at twenty-two stone. The-man-who-won't-give-his-name has a big tough face with a broken nose. Hair grows from him everywhere, it issues from his nose, his ears, flourishes in big bushy white eyebrows, on his hands, his fingers and, Finch has noticed, on his large rounded back. He is the only original tenant. It was because of him that Florence Nightingale suggested the place to Fantoni, thinking he would find a friend in another fat man. Fantoni offered accommodation to Milligan. A month or so later Finch and May were strolling along 16 October Avenue (once known as Royal Parade) when they saw three men talking on the upstairs balcony outside Fantoni's room. Fantoni waved. May waved back, Milligan called to them to come up, and they did. Glino moved in a week later, having been sent with a letter of introduction from Florence Nightingale.

It was Fantoni who devised the now legendary scheme for removing the other tenants. And although the-man-who-won't-give-his-name never participated in the scheme, he never interfered or reported the matter to the authorities.

The-man-who-won't-give-his-name says little and keeps to himself. But he always says good morning and goodnight and once discussed Iceland with Finch on the day Finch brought home the map. Finch believes he was a sailor, but Fantoni claims that he is Calsen, an academic who was kicked out of the university for seducing one of "the little scrawnies".

Finch stands in front of the mirror, his hands digging into his stomach. He wonders what Fantoni would say if he knew that Finch had been engaged to two diminutive girls, Deidre and Anne, fragile girls with the slender arms of children who had both loved him with a total and unreasonable love, and he them, before the revolution.

4

May turns his Sibelius record to side two and begins one more letter to his wife. He begins, Dear Iris, just a short note to say everything is all right.

5

Finch is sitting in the kitchen leafing through the Botticelli book he has just bought. It took half the pension money. Everyone is

14

out. He turns each page gently, loving the expensive paper as much as the reproductions.

Behind him he hears the key in the front door. He puts the book in the cupboard under the sink, among the saucepans, and begins to wash up the milk bottles; there are dozens of them, all dirty, all stinking.

There is cursing and panting in the passage. He can hear Fantoni saying, the little weed, the little fucker. Glino says something. There is an unusual sense of urgency in their voices. They both come into the kitchen at once. Their clothes are covered with dirt but Fantoni is wearing overalls.

Glino says, we went out to Deer Park.

There is an explosives factory at Deer Park. Fantoni has discussed it for months. No one could tell him what sort of explosive they made out there, but he was convinced it was dynamite.

Fantoni pushes Finch away from the sink and begins to wash the dirt off his hands and face. He says, the little weeds had guns.

Finch looks at Glino who is leaning against the door with his eyes closed, his hands opening and closing. He is trembling. There is a small scratch on one of his round, smooth cheeks and blood is seeping through his transparent skin. He says, I thought I was going in again, I thought we'd gone for sure.

Fantoni says, shut-up Glino.

Glino says, Christ, if you've ever been inside one of those places you'll never want to see one again.

He is talking about prison. The fright seems to have overcome some of his shyness. He says, Christ I couldn't stand it.

Finch, handing Fantoni a tea towel to dry himself with, says, did you get the dynamite?

Fantoni says, well, what do *you* think! It's past your bed time.

Finch leaves, worrying about the Botticelli book.

6

Florence Nightingale will soon be here to collect the rents. Officially she arrives at 8 p.m., but at 7.30 she will arrive secretly, entering through the backyard, and visit Finch in "the new extensions".

Finch has showered early and shaved carefully. And he waits in his room, the door closed for privacy, checking with nervous eyes to see that everything is tidy.

These visits are never mentioned to the others, there is an unspoken understanding that they never will be.

There is a small tap on the door and Florence Nightingale enters, smiling shyly. She says, wow, the heat. She is wearing a simple yellow dress and leather sandals that lace up her calves Roman style. She closes the door with an exaggerated sort of care and tip-toes across to Finch who is standing, his face wreathed in a large smile.

She says, hello Cuddles, and kisses him on the cheek. Finch embraces her and pats her gently on the back. He says, the heat . . .

As usual Finch sits on the bed and Florence Nightingale squats yoga style on the goatskin rug at his feet. Finch once said, you look as if Modigliani painted you. And was pleased that she knew of Modigliani and was flattered by the comparison. She has a long straight face with a nose that is long vertically but not horizontally. Her teeth are straight and perfect, but a little on the long side. But now they are not visible and her lips are closed in a strange calm smile that suggests melancholy. They enjoy their melancholy together, Finch and Florence Nightingale. Her eyes, which are grey, are very big and very wide and she looks around the room as she does each time, looking for new additions.

She says, it got to 103 degrees . . . the steering wheel was too hot to touch.

Finch says, I was shopping. I got a book on Botticelli.

Her eyes begin to circle the room more quickly. She says, where, show me?

Finch giggles. He says, it's in the kitchen cupboard. Fantoni came back while I was reading it.

She says, you shouldn't be frightened of Fantoni, he won't eat you. You've got blue sheets, *double* blue sheets. She raises her eyebrows.

He says, no significance, it was just the colour.

She says, I don't believe you. *Double* blue sheets. Florence Nightingale likes to invent a secret love life for him but he doesn't know why. But they enjoy this, this sexual/asexual flirtation.

16

Finch is never sure what it is meant to be but he has never had any real hopes regarding Florence Nightingale, although in sleep and half-sleep he has made love to her many times. She is not quite frail enough. There is a strength that she attempts to hide with little girl's shyness. And sometimes there is a strange awkwardness in her movements as if some logical force in her mind is trying to deny the grace of her body. She sits on the floor, her head cocked characteristically on one side so her long hair falls over one eye. She says, how's the Freedom Fighter?

The Freedom Fighter was Finch's name for Fantoni. Finch says, oh nothing, we haven't done anything yet, just plans.

She says, I drove past the 16 October Statue—it's still there.

Finch says, we can't get the explosive. Maybe we'll just paint it yellow.

Florence Nightingale says, maybe you should eat it.

Finch loves that. He says, that's good, Nancy, that's really good.

Florence Nightingale says, it's your role isn't it? The eaters? You should behave in character, the way they expect you to. You should eat everything. Eat the Committee of Seventy-five. She is rocking back and forth on the floor holding her knees, balancing on her arse.

Finch tries not to look up her skirt. He says, a feast.

She cups her hands to make a megaphone and says, The Fat Men Against The Revolution have eaten General Kooper.

He says, and General Alvarez.

She says, the Central Emporium was devoured last night, huge droppings have been discovered in 16 October Avenue.

He says, you make me feel like the old days, good fat, not bad fat.

She says, I've got to go. I was late tonight. I brought you some cigars, some extra ones for you.

She has jumped up, kissed him, and departed before he has time to thank her. He remains on the bed, nursing some vague disappointment, staring at the goatskin rug.

Slowly he smiles to himself, thinking about eating the October 16 Statue.

7

Florence Nightingale will soon be here to collect the rents. With the exception of Fantoni, who is in the shower, and Glino, who is cooking his vegetarian meal in his little cupboard, everyone is in the kitchen.

Finch sits on a kerosene drum by the back annexe, hoping to catch whatever breeze may come through.

Milligan, in very tight blue shorts, yellow T-shirt, and blue-tinted glasses, squats beside him smiling to himself and rubbing his hands together. He has just finished telling a very long and involved story about a prostitute he picked up in his cab and who paid him double to let her conduct her business in the back seat. She made him turn his mirror back to front. No one cares if the story is true or not.

Milligan says, yep.

Milligan wears his clothes like corsets, always too tight. He says it is good for his blood, the tightness. But his flesh erupts in strange bulges from his thighs and stomach and arms. He looks trussed up, a grinning turkey ready for the oven.

Milligan always has a story. His life is a continual charade, a collection of prostitutes and criminals, "characters", beautiful women, eccentric old ladies, homosexuals, and two-headed freaks. Also he knows many jokes. Finch and May sit on the velvet cushions in Milligan's room and listen to the stories, but it is bad for May who becomes depressed. The evenings invariably end with May in a fury saying, Jesus, I want a fuck, I want a fuck so badly it hurts. But Milligan just keeps laughing, somehow never realizing how badly it affects May.

May, Finch, Milligan, and the-man-who-won't-give-his-name lounge around the kitchen drinking Glino's homemade beer. Finch has suggested that they wash the dirty milk bottles before Florence Nightingale arrives and everyone has agreed that it is a good idea. However they have all remained seated, drinking Glino's homemade beer. No one likes the beer, but of all the things that are hard to steal alcohol is the hardest. Even Fantoni cannot arrange it. Once he managed to get hold of a nine-gallon keg of beer but it sat in the back yard for a year before Glino got hold of a gas cylinder and the gear for pumping it out. They were drunk for one and a half days on that lot, and were nearly arrested en masse when they went out to piss on the commemorative plaque outside the offices of the Fifty-fourth District.

No one says much. They sip Glino's beer from jam jars and look around the room as if considering ways to tidy it, removing the milk bottles, doing something about the rubbish bin—a cardboard box which was full a week ago and from which eggshells, tins, and breadcrusts cascade on to the floor. Every now and then May reads something from an old newspaper, laughing very loudly. When May laughs, Finch smiles. He is happy to see May laughing because when he is not laughing he is very sad and liable to break things and do himself an injury. May's forehead is still scarred from the occasion when he battered it against the front door for three hours. There is still blood on the paintwork.

May wears an overcoat all the time, even tonight in this heat. His form is amorphous. He has a double chin and a drooping face that hangs downwards from his nose. He is balding and worries about losing hair. He sleeps for most of the day to escape his depression and spends the nights walking around the house, drinking endless glasses of water, playing his record, and groaning to himself as he tries to sleep.

May is the only one who was married before the revolution. He came to this town when he was fired from his job as a refrigerator salesman, and his wife was to join him later. Now he can't find her. She has sold their house and he is continually writing letters to her, care of anyone he can think of who might know her whereabouts.

May is also in love with Florence Nightingale, and in this respect he is no different from the other five, even Fantoni who claims to find her skinny and undernourished.

Florence Nightingale is their friend, their confidante, their rent collector, their mascot. She works for the revolution but is against it. She will be here soon. Everybody is waiting for her. They talk about what she will wear.

Milligan, staring intently at his large Omega watch, says, peep, peep, peep, on the third stroke . . .

The front door bell rings. It is Florence Nightingale.

The-man-who-won't-give-his-name springs up. He says, I'll get it, I'll get it. He looks very serious but his broken, battered face appears to be very gentle. He says, I'll get it. And sounds

19

out of breath. He moves with fast heavy strides, along the passage, his back hunched urgently like a jungle animal, a rhino, ploughing through undergrowth. It is rumoured that he is having an affair with Florence Nightingale but it doesn't seem possible.

They crowd together in the small kitchen, their large soft bodies crammed together around the door. When Florence Nightingale nears the door there is much pushing and shoving and Milligan dances around the outside of the crowd, unable to get through, crying "Make way there, make way for the lady with the big blue eyes" in his high nasal voice, and everyone pushes every way at once. Finally it is Fantoni who arrives from his shower and says, "For Christ's sake, give a man some *room*'.

Everybody is very silent. They don't like to hear him swear in front of Florence Nightingale. Only Fantoni would do it, no one else. Now he nods to her and indicates that she should sit down on one of the two chairs. Fantoni takes the other. For the rest there are packing cases, kerosene tins, and an empty beer keg which is said to cause piles.

Fantoni is wearing a new safari suit, but no one mentions it. He has sewn insignia on the sleeves and the epaulettes. No one has ever seen this insignia before. No one mentions it. They pretend Fantoni is wearing his white wool suit as usual.

Florence Nightingale sits simply with her hands folded in her lap. She greets them all by name and in turn; to the-man-who-won't-give-his-name she merely says "Hello". But it is not difficult to see that there is something between them. The-man-who-won't-give-his-name shuffles his large feet and suddenly smiles very broadly. He says, "Hello".

Fantoni then collects the rent which they pay from their pensions. The rent is not large, but the pensions are not large either. Only Milligan has an income, which gives him a certain independence.

Finch doesn't have enough for the rent. He had meant to borrow the difference from Milligan but forgot. Now he is too embarrassed to ask in front of Fantoni.

He says, I'm a bit short.

Florence Nightingale says, forget it, try and get it for next week. She counts the money and gives everyone a receipt. Finch tries to catch Milligan's eye.

Later, when everyone is smoking the cigars she has brought and drinking Glino's home brew, she says, I hate this job, it's horrible to take this money from you.

Glino is sitting on the beer keg. He says, what job would you like? But he doesn't look at Florence Nightingale. Glino never looks at anyone.

Florence Nightingale says, I would come and look after you. We could all live together and I'd cook you crêpes suzettes.

And Fantoni says, but who would bring us cigars then? And everybody laughs.

8

Everyone is a little bit drunk.

Florence Nightingale says, Glino play us a tune.

Glino says nothing, but seems to double up even more so that his broad shoulders become one with his large bay window. His fine white hair falls over his face.

Everybody says, come on Glino, give us a tune. Until, finally, Glino takes his mouth organ from his back pocket and, without once looking up, begins to play. He plays something very slow. It reminds Finch of an albatross, an albatross flying over a vast, empty ocean. The albatross is going nowhere. Glino's head is so bowed that no one can see the mouth organ, it is sandwiched between his nose and his chest. Only his pink, translucent hands move slowly from side to side.

Then, as if changing its mind, the albatross becomes a gipsy, a pedlar, or a drunken troubador. Glino's head shakes, his foot taps, his hands dance.

Milligan jumps to his feet. He dances a sailor's dance, Finch thinks it might be the hornpipe, or perhaps it is his own invention, like the pink stars stencilled on his taxi door. Milligan has a happy, impish face with eyebrows that rise and fall from behind his blue-tinted glasses. If he weighed less his face might even be pretty. Milligan's face is half-serious, half-mocking, intent on the dance, and Florence Nightingale stands slowly. They both dance, Florence Nightingale whirling and turning, her hair flying, her eyes nearly closed. The music becomes faster and faster and the five fat men move back to stand against the wall, as if flung there by centrifugal force. Finch, pulling the table out of the way, feels he will lose his balance. Milligan's face is bright red and streaming with sweat. The flesh on his bare white thighs shifts and shakes and beneath his T-shirt his breasts move up and down. Suddenly he spins to one side, drawn to the edge of the room, and collapses in a heap on the floor.

Everyone claps. Florence Nightingale keeps dancing. The clapping is forced into the rhythm of the music and everyone claps in time. May is dancing with Florence Nightingale. His movements are staccato, he stands with his feet apart, his huge overcoat flapping, slaps his thighs, claps his hands together above his head, stamps his feet, spins, jumps, shouts, nearly falls, takes Florence Nightingale around the waist and spins her around and around, they both stumble, but neither stop. May's face is transformed, it is living. The teeth in his partly open mouth shine white. His overcoat is like some magical cloak, a swirling beautiful thing.

Florence Nightingale constantly sweeps long hair out of her eyes.

May falls. Finch takes his place but becomes puffed very quickly and gives over to the-man-who-won't-give-his-name.

The-man-who-won't-give-his-name takes Florence Nightingale in his arms and disregards the music. He begins a very slow, gliding waltz. Milligan whispers in Glino's ear. Glino looks up shyly for a moment, pauses, then begins to play a Strauss waltz.

Finch says, the "Blue Danube". To no one in particular.

The-man-who-won't-give-his-name dances beautifully and very proudly. He holds Florence Nightingale slightly away from him, his head is high and cocked to one side. Florence Nightingale whispers something in his ear. He looks down at her and raises his eyebrows. They waltz around and around the kitchen until Finch becomes almost giddy with embarrassment. He thinks, it is like a wedding.

Glino once said (of prisons), "If you've ever been inside one of those places you wouldn't ever want to be inside one again."

Tonight Finch can see him lying on his bunk in a cell, playing the "Blue Danube" and the albatross and staring at the ceiling. He wonders if it is so very different from that now: they spend their days lying on their beds, afraid to go out because they don't like the way people look at them.

The dancing finishes and the-man-who-won't-give-his-name escorts Florence Nightingale to her chair. He is so large, he treats her as if she were wrapped in crinkly cellophane, a gentleman holding flowers.

Milligan earns his own money. He asks Fantoni, why don't you dance?

Fantoni is leaning against the wall smoking another cigar. He looks at Milligan for a long time until Finch is convinced that Fantoni will punch Milligan.

Finally Fantoni says, I can't dance.

9

They all walk up the passage with Florence Nightingale. Approaching the front door she drops an envelope. The envelope spins gently to the floor and everyone walks around it. They stand on the porch and wave goodnight to her as she drives off in her black government car.

Returning to the house Milligan stoops and picks up the envelope. He hands it to Finch and says, for you. Inside the official envelope is a form letter with the letterhead of the Department of Housing. It says, Dear Mr. Finch, the department regrets that you are now in arrears with your rent. If this matter is not settled within the statutory seven days you will be required to find other accommodation. It is signed, Nancy Bowlby.

Milligan says, what is it?

Finch says, it's from Florence Nightingale, about the rent.

Milligan says, seven days?

Finch says, oh, she has a job to do, it's not her fault.

10

May has the back room upstairs. Finch is lying in bed in "the new extensions". He can hear Milligan calling to May.

Milligan says, May?

May says, what is it?

Milligan says, come here.

Their voices, Milligan's distant, May's close, seem to exist only inside Finch's head.

May says, what do you want?

Milligan shouts, I want to tell you something.

May says, no you don't, you just want me to tuck you in.
Milligan says, no. No, I don't.

Fantoni's loud raucous laugh comes from even further away.

The-man-who-won't-give-his-name is knocking on the ceiling
of his room with a broom. Finch can hear it going, bump, bump,
bump. The Sibelius record jumps. May shouts, quit it.

Milligan says, I want to tell you something.

May shouts, no you don't.

Finch lies naked on top of the blue sheets and tries to hum the
albatross song but he has forgotten it.

Milligan says, come *here*. May? May, I want to tell you something.

May says, tuck yourself in, you lazy bugger.

Milligan giggles. The giggle floats out into the night.

Fantoni is in helpless laughter.

Milligan says, May?

May's footsteps echo across the floorboards of his room and
cross the corridor to Milligan's room. Finch hears Milligan's
laughter and hears May's footsteps returning to May's room.

Fantoni shouts, what did he want?

May says, he wanted to be tucked in.

Fantoni laughs. May turns up the Sibelius record. The-man-
who-won't-give-his-name knocks on the ceiling with a broom.
The record jumps.

11

It is 4 a.m. and not yet light. No one can see them. As May and
Finch leave the house a black government car draws away from
the kerb but, although both of them see it, neither mentions it.

At 4 a.m. it is cool and pleasant to walk through the waste
lands surrounding the house. There are one or two lights on in
the big blocks of flats, but everyone seems to be asleep.

They walk slowly, picking their way through the thistles.

Finally May says, you were crazy.

Finch says, I know.

They walk for a long time. Finch wonders why the thistles

grow in these parts, why they are sad, why they only grow where the ground has been disturbed, and wonders where they grew originally.

He says, do they make you sad?

May says, what?

He says, the thistles.

May doesn't answer. Finally he says, you were crazy to mention it. He'll really do it. He'll *really* do it.

Finch stubs his toe on a large block of concrete. The pain seems deserved. He says, it didn't enter my mind—that he'd think of Nancy.

May says, he'll really do it. He'll bloody-well eat her. Christ, you know what he's like.

Finch says, I know, but I didn't mention Nancy, just the statue.

May wraps his overcoat around himself and draws his head down into it. He says, he *looks* evil, he *likes* being fat.

Finch says, that's reasonable.

May says, I can still remember what it was like being thin. Did I tell you, I was only six, but I can remember it like it was yesterday. Jesus it was nice. Although I don't suppose I appreciated it at the time.

Finch says, shut-up.

May says, he's still trying to blow up that bloody statue and he'll get caught. Probably blow himself up. Then we'll be the ones that have to pinch everything. And we'll get caught, or we'll starve more like it.

Finch says, help him get some dynamite and then dob him in to the cops. While he's in jail he couldn't eat Florence Nightingale.

May says, and we wouldn't eat anything. I wouldn't mind so much if he just wanted to screw her. I wouldn't mind screwing her myself.

Finch says, maybe he is. Already.

May pulls his overcoat tightly around himself and says, no, it's whatshisname, the big guy, that's who's screwing her. Did you see them dancing? It's him.

Finch says, I like him.

May says nothing. They have come near a main road and they

wordlessly turn back, keeping away from the street lights, returning to the thistles.

Finch says, it was Nancy's idea. She said why don't we eat the statue.

May says, you told me already. You were nuts. She was nuts too but she was only joking. You should have known that he's serious about everything. He really wants to blow up everything, not just the fucking statue.

Finch says, he's a fascist.

May says, what's a facist?

Finch says, like Danko . . . like General Kooper . . . like Fantoni. He's going to dig a hole in the backyard. He calls it the barbecue.

12

In another two hours Finch will have earned enough money for the rent. Fantoni is paying him by the hour. In another two hours he will be clear and then he'll stop. He hopes there is still two hours' work. They are digging a hole among the dock weeds in the backyard. It is a trench like a grave but only three feet deep. He asked Milligan for the money but Milligan had already lent money to Glino and May.

Fantoni is wearing a pair of May's trousers so he won't get his own dirty. He is stripped to the waist and working with a mattock. Finch clears the earth Fantoni loosens; he has a long-handled shovel. Both the shovel and the mattock are new, they have appeared miraculously, like anything that Fantoni wants.

They have chosen a spot outside Finch's window, where it is completely private, shielded from the neighbouring houses. It is a small private spot which Fantoni normally uses for sunbathing.

The top of Fantoni's bristly head is bathed in sweat and small dams of sweat have caught in the creases on the back of his head; he gives strange grunts between swings and carries out a conversation with Finch who is too exhausted to answer.

He says, I want the whole thing . . . in writing, OK? . . . write it down . . . all the reasons . . . just like you explained it to me.

Finch is getting less and less earth on the shovel. He keeps aiming at the earth and overshooting it, collecting a few loose clods on the blade. He says, yes.

Fantoni takes the shovel from him. He says, you write that now, write all the reasons like you told me and I'll count that as time working. How's that?

And he pats Finch on the back.

Finch is not sure how it is. He cannot believe any of it. He cannot believe that he, Alexander Finch, is digging a barbecue to cook a beautiful girl called Florence Nightingale in the backyard of a house in what used to be called Royal Parade. He would not have believed it, and still cannot.

He says, thanks Fantoni.

Fantoni says, what I want, Finch is a thing called a rationale . . . that's the word isn't it . . . they're called rationales.

13

Rationale by A. Finch

The following is a suggested plan of action for the "Fat Men Against The Revolution".

It is suggested that the Fat Men of this establishment pursue a course of militant love, by bodily consuming a senior member of the revolution, an official of the revolution, or a monument of the revolution (e.g. the 16 October Statue).

Such an act would, in the eyes of the revolution, be in character. The Fat Men of this society have been implicitly accused of (among other things) loving food too much, of loving themselves too much to the exclusion of the revolution. To eat a member or monument of the revolution could be seen as a way of turning this love towards the revolution. Eating is a total and literal act of consummation. The Fat Men would incorporate in their own bodies all that could be good and noble in the revolution and excrete that which is bad. In other words, the bodies of Fat Men will purify the revolution.

Alexander Finch shivers violently although it is very hot. He makes a fair copy of the draft. When he has finished he goes upstairs to the toilet and tries, unsuccessfully, to vomit.

Fantoni is supervising the delivery of a load of wood, coke, and kindling in the backyard. He is dressed beautifully in a white suit made from lightweight wool. He is smoking one of Florence Nightingale's cigars.

As Finch descends the stairs he hears a loud shout and then, two steps later, a loud crash. It came from May's room. And Finch knows without looking that May has thrown his bowl of goldfish against the wall. May loved his goldfish.

14

At dinner Finch watches Fantoni eat the omelette that Glino has cooked for him. Fantoni cuts off dainty pieces. He buries the dainty pieces in the small fleshy orifice beneath his large moustache.

15

May wakes him at 2 a.m. He says, I've just realized where she is. She'll be with her brother. That's where she'll be. I wrote her a letter.

Finch says, Florence Nightingale.

May says, my wife.

16

Glino knows. Milligan knows. May and Finch know. Only the-man-who-won't-give-his-name is unaware of the scheme. He asked Fantoni about the hole in the backyard. Fantoni said, it is a wigwam for a goose's bridle.

17

The deputation moves slowly on tip-toes from Finch's room. In the kitchen annexe someone trips over Fantoni's bicycle. It crashes. Milligan giggles. Finch punches him sharply in the ribs. In the dark, Milligan's face is caught between laughter and surprise. He pushes his glasses back on the bridge of his nose and peers closely at Finch.

The others have continued and are now moving quietly through the darkened kitchen. Finch pats Milligan on the shoulder. He whispers, I'm sorry. But Milligan passes on to join the others where they huddle nervously outside the-man-who-won't-give-his-name's room.

Glino looks to Finch, who moves through them and slowly opens the door. Finch sums up the situation. He feels a dull soft shock. He stops, but the others push him into the room. Only when they are all assembled inside the room, very close to the door, does everybody realize that the-man-who-won't-give-his-name is in bed with Florence Nightingale.

Florence Nightingale is lying on her side, facing the door, attempting to smile. The-man-who-won't-give-his-name is climbing from the bed. Finch is shocked to see that he is still wearing his socks. For some reason this makes everything worse.

The-man-who-won't-give-his-name seems very slow and very old. He rummages through the pile of clothes beside the bed, his breathing the only sound in the room. It is hoarse, heavy breathing that only subsides after he has found his underpants. He trips getting into them and Finch notices they are on inside out. Eventually the-man-who-won't-give-his-name says, it is generally considered good manners to knock.

He begins to dress now. No one knows what to do. They watch him hand Florence Nightingale her items of clothing so she can dress beneath the sheet. He sits in front of her then, partially obscuring her struggles. Florence Nightingale is no longer trying to smile. She looks very sad, almost frightened.

Eventually Finch says, this is more important, I'm afraid, more important than knocking on doors.

He has accepted some new knowledge and the acceptance makes him feel strong although he has no real idea of what the knowledge is. He says, Fantoni is planning to eat Florence Nightingale.

Florence Nightingale, struggling with her bra beneath the sheet, says, we know, we were discussing it.

Milligan giggles.

The-man-who-won't-give-his-name has found his dressing-gown in the cupboard in the corner. He remains there, like a boxer waiting between rounds.

Florence Nightingale is staring at her yellow dress on the floor. Glino and May bump into each other as they reach for it at the same moment. They both retreat and both step forward again. Finally it is Milligan who darts forward, picks up the garment, and hands it to Florence Nightingale, who disappears under the sheets once more. Finch finds it almost impossible not to stare at her. He wishes she would come out and dress quickly and get the whole thing over and done with.

Technically, Florence Nightingale has deceived no one.

Glino says, we got to stop him.

Florence Nightingale's head appears from beneath the sheets. She smiles at them all. She says, you are all wonderful . . . I love you all.

It is the first time Finch has ever heard Florence Nightingale say anything so insincere or so false. He wishes she would unsay that.

Finch says, he must be stopped.

Behind him he can hear a slight shuffling. He looks around to see May, his face flushed red, struggling to keep the door closed. He makes wild signs with his eyes to indicate that someone is trying to get in. Finch leans against the door, which pushes back with the heavy weight of a dream. Florence Nightingale slides sideways out of bed and Glino pushes against Finch, who is sandwiched between two opposing forces. Finally it is the-man-who-won't-give-his-name who says, let him in.

Everybody steps back, but the door remains closed. They stand grouped in a semi-circle around it, waiting. For a moment it seems as if it was all a mistake. But, finally, the door knob turns and the door is pushed gently open. Fantoni stands in the doorway wearing white silk pyjamas.

He says, what's this, an orgy?

No one knows what to do or say.

18
Glino is still vomiting in the drain in the backyard. He has been vomiting since dawn and it is now dark. Finch said he should be let off, because he was a vegetarian, but the-man-who-won't-give-his-name insisted. So they made Glino eat just a little bit.

The stench hangs heavily over the house.

May is playing his record.

Finch has thought many times that he might also vomit.

The blue sheet which was used to strangle Fantoni lies in a long tangled line from the kitchen through the kitchen annexe and out into the backyard, where Glino lies retching and where the barbecue pit, although filled in, still smokes slowly, the smoke rising from the dry earth.

The-man-who-won't-give-his-name had his dressing-gown ruined. It was soaked with blood. He sits in the kitchen now, wearing Fantoni's white safari suit. He sits reading Fantoni's mail. He has suggested that it would be best if he were referred to as Fantoni, should the police come, and that anyway it would be best if he were referred to as Fantoni. A bottle of scotch sits on the table beside him. It is open to anyone, but so far only May has taken any.

Finch is unable to sleep. He has tried to sleep but can see only Fantoni's face. He steps over Glino and enters the kitchen.

He says, may I have a drink please, Fantoni?

It is a relief to be able to call him a name.

19

The-man-who-won't-give-his-name has taken up residence in Fantoni's room. Everybody has become used to him now. He is known as Fantoni.

A new man has also arrived, being sent by Florence Nightingale with a letter of introduction. So far his name is unknown.

20

"*Revolution in a Closed Society—A Study of Leadership among the Fat*"
By Nancy Bowlby

Leaders were selected for their ability to provide materially for the welfare of the group as a whole. Obviously the same qualities should reside in the heir-apparent, although these qualities were not always obvious during the waiting period; for this reason I judged it necessary to show favouritism to the heir-apparent and thus to raise his prestige in the eyes of the group. This favouritism would sometimes take the form of small gifts and, in those rare cases where it was needed, shows of physical affection as well.

A situation of "crisis" was occasionally triggered, *deus ex machina*, by suggestion, but usually arose spontaneously and had only to be encouraged. From this point on, as I shall discuss later in this paper, the "revolution" took a similar course and "Fantoni" was always disposed of effectively and the new "Fantoni" took control of the group.

The following results were gathered from a study of twenty-three successive "Fantonis". Apart from the "Fantoni" and the "Fantoni-apparent", the composition of the group remained unaltered. Whilst it can be admitted that studies so far are at an early stage, the results surely justify the continuation of the experiments with larger groups.

Peeling

She moves around the house on soft slow feet, her footsteps padding softly above me as I lie, on my unmade bed of unwashed sheets, listening. She knows, as she always knows, that I am listening to her and it is early morning. The fog has not risen. The traffic crawls outside. There is a red bus, I can see the top of it, outside the window. If I cared to look more closely I could see the faces of the people in the bus, and, with luck, my own reflection, or, at least, the reflection of my white hair, my one distinction. The mail has not yet arrived. There will be nothing for me, but I wait for it. Life is nothing without expectation. I am always first to pick up the letters when they drop through the door. The milk bottles, two days old, are in the kitchen unwashed and she knows this too, because she has not yet come.

Our relationship is beyond analysis. It was Bernard, although I prefer to name no names, who suggested that the relationship had a boyscout flavour about it. So much he knows. Bernard, who travels halfway across London to find the one priest who will forgive his incessant masturbation, cannot be regarded as an authority in this matter.

Outside the fog is thick, the way it is always meant to be in London, but seldom is, unless you live by the river, which I don't. Today will not disappoint the American tourists.

And she walks above my head, probably arranging the little white dolls which she will not explain and which I never ask about, knowing she will not explain, and not for the moment wishing an explanation. She buys the dolls from the Portobello Road, the north end, on Friday morning, and at another market on Thursdays, she has not revealed where, but leaves early, at about 5 a.m. I know it is a market she goes to, but I don't know which one. The dolls arrive in all conditions, crammed into a large cardboard suitcase which she takes out on her expeditions. Those which still have hair she plucks bald, and those with eyes lose them, and those with teeth have them removed and she paints them, slowly, white. She uses a flat plastic paint. I have seen the tins.

She arranges the dolls in unexpected places. So that, walking up the stairs a little drunk, one might be confronted with a collection of bald white dolls huddled together in a swarm. Her room, which was once my room, she has painted white; the babies merge into its walls and melt into the bedspread which is also white. White, which has become a fashionable colour of late, has no appeal to her, it is simply that it says nothing, being less melodramatic than black.

I must admit that I loathe white. I would prefer a nice blue, a pretty blue, like a blue sky. A powder blue, I think it is called. Or an eggshell blue. Something a little more feminine. Something with—what do you call it—more character about it. When I finally take her to bed (and I am in no hurry, no hurry at all) I will get some better idea of her true colour, get under her skin as it were.

Did you get the pun?

I have found her, on numerous occasions, playing Monopoly in the middle of her room, drinking Guinness, surrounded by white dolls.

Several times a week she comes to wash my dishes and to be persuaded to share a meal with me. The consumption of food is, for the moment, our most rewarding mutual occupation. We discuss, sometimes, the experience of the flavours. We talk about the fish fingers or the steak and kidney pies from Marks & Sparks. She is still shy, and needs to be coaxed. She has revealed to me a love for oysters which I find exciting. Each week I put a little of my pension aside. When I have enough I will buy oysters and we will discuss them in detail. I often think of this meal.

An an earlier stage I did not understand myself so well, and achieved, on one or two occasions, a quiet drunken kiss. But I have not pursued the matter, being content, for the moment, with the meals and the company on these quiet nights now that the television has been taken away and now that I, unemployed, have so little money to spend with the ladies in Bayswater, the cinema, or even a pint of best bitter in the Bricklayers Arms which, to tell the truth, I always found dull.

I am in no hurry. There is no urgency in the matter. Sooner or later we shall discuss the oysters. Then it will be time to move on to other more intimate things, moving layer after layer, until I discover her true colours, her flavours, her smells. The prospects of so slow an exploration excites me and I am in no hurry, no hurry at all. May it last forever.

Let me describe my darling. Shall I call her that? An adventure I had planned to keep, but now it is said. Let me describe her to you. My darling has a long pale face with long golden hair, slightly frizzy, the kind with odd waving pieces that catch the light and look pretty. Her nose is long, downwards, not outwards, making her appear more sorrowful than she might be. Her breasts, I would guess, are large and heavy, but she wears so many sweaters (for want of a better term) that it is hard to tell; likewise the subtleties of her figure. But she moves, my darling, with the grace of a cat, pacing about her room surrounded by her white dolls and her Monopoly money.

She seems to have no job and I have never asked her about her occupation. That is still to come, many episodes later. I shall record it if and when it is revealed. For the moment: she keeps no regular hours, none that I can equate with anything. But I, for that matter, keep no regular hours either and, never having owned a clock, have been timeless since the battery in the transistor radio gave out. Normally it seems to be late afternoon.

She is making up her mind. I can hear her at the top of the stairs. Twice, in the last few minutes, she has come out on to the landing and then retreated back into her room. She has walked around her room. She has stood by the window. Now she moves towards the landing once more. She is there. There is a silence. Perhaps she is arranging dolls on the landing.

No. She is, I think, I am almost positive, descending the stairs, on tip-toe. She plans to surprise me.

A tap at the door. My stomach rumbles.

I move quickly to the door and open it. She says hello, and smiles in a tired way.

She says, phew. (She is referring to the smell of the bad milk in the unwashed bottles.)

I apologize, smooth down my bed, pull up the cover, and offer her a place to sit. She accepts, throwing my pyjama pants under the bed for the sake of tidiness.

She says, how is your situation.

I relate the state of the employment market. But she, I notice, is a little fidgety. She plays with the corner of the sheet. She is distracted, appears to be impatient. I continue with my report but know she is not fully listening.

She leaves the bed and begins to wash up, heating the water on the small gas heater. I ask her of her situation but she remains silent.

The water is not yet hot enough but she pours it into the tub and begins to wash up, moving slowly and quickly at the same time. I dry. I ask her of her situation.

She discusses George who I am unsure of. He was possibly her husband. It appears there was a child. The child she visits every third Sunday. For the hundredth time I remark on how unreasonable this is. The conversation tells neither of us anything, but then that is not its purpose. The dishes she dispenses with quickly, an untidy washer, I could do better myself—she leaves large portions of food behind on plates, bottles, and cutlery, but I do not complain—I keep the dishes to attract her, like honey.

I relate a slightly risqué joke, a joke so old it is new to her. She laughs beautifully, her head thrown back, her long white throat like the throat of a white doll, but soft, like the inside of a thigh. Her throat is remarkable, her voice coming softly from it, timorously, pianissimo.

She is, how to call it, artistic. She wears the clothes of an ordinary person, of a great number of quite different ordinary persons, but she arranges them in the manner of those who are called artistic. Small pieces of things are tacked together with a confidence that contradicts her manner and amazes me. Pieces of tiny artificial flowers, a part of a butcher's apron, old Portuguese boots, a silver pendant, medal ribbons, a hand-painted stole, and a hundred milk bottle tops made unrecognizable. She is like a magpie with a movable nest.

Her name, which I had earlier decided not to reveal, is Nile.

It is too private a name to reveal. But it is so much a part of her that I feel loath to change it for fear I will leave something important out. Not to mention it would be like forgetting to mention the white dolls.

The washing-up is finished and it is too early yet to prepare a meal. It is a pleasant time, a time of expectation. It needs, like all things, the greatest control. But I am an expert in these matters, a man who can make a lump of barley sugar last all day.

We sit side by side on the bed and read the papers. I take the employment section and she, as usual, the deaths, births, and marriages. As usual she reads them all, her pale nail-bitten finger moving slowly over the columns of type, her lips moving silently as she reads the names.

She says, half to herself, they never put them in.

I am at once eager and reluctant to pick up this thread. I am not sure if it is a loose thread or one that might, so to speak, unravel the whole sweater. I wait, no longer seeing the words I am looking at. My ear drums are so finely stretched that I fear they may burst.

She says, don't you think they should put them in?

My stomach rumbles loudly. I say, what? And find my voice, normally so light, husky and cracked.

She says, babies . . . abortion babies . . . they're unlisted.

As I feared it is not a loose thread, but the other kind. Before she says more I can sense that she is about to reveal more than she should at this stage. I am disappointed in her. I thought she knew the rules.

I would like, for the sake of politeness, to answer her, but I am anxious and unable to say any more. I do not, definitely not, wish to know, at this stage, why she should have this interest in abortion babies. I find her behaviour promiscuous.

She says, do you think they have souls?

I turn to look at her, surprised by the unusual pleading tone in her voice, a voice which is normally so inexpressive. Looking at her eyes I feel I am being drowned in milk.

She pins back a stray wisp of hair with a metal pin. I say, I have never thought of the matter.

She says, don't be huffy.

I say, I am not huffy.

But that is not entirely correct. Let us say, I am put out. If I had any barley sugar left I would give her a piece, then I would instruct her in the art of sucking barley sugar, the patience that is needed to make it last, the discipline that is required to forget the teeth, to use only the tongue. But I have no barley sugar.

I say, I am old, but it will be a little while before I die.

She says (surprisingly), you are so morbid.

We sit for a little while quite silently, both looking at our pieces of newspapers. I am not reading mine, because I know that she is not reading hers. She is going to bring up the subject again.

Instead she says, I have never told you what I do.

Another thread, but this one seems a little less drastic. It suits me nicely. I would prefer to know these things, the outside layers, before we come to the centre of things.

I say, no, what do you do?

She says, I help do abortions.

She may as well have kicked me in the stomach, I would have preferred it. She has come back to the abortion again. I did not wish to discuss anything so . . . deep?

I say, we all have our jobs to do, should we be so lucky as to have a job, which as you know . . .

She says, the abortionist is not a doctor, there are a number of rooms around London, sometimes at Shepherd's Bush, Notting Hill, there is one at Wimbledon, a large house.

I have not heard of this sort of thing before. I examine her hands. They are small and pale with closely bitten nails and one or two faintly pink patches around the knuckles. I ask her if she wears rubber gloves. She says yes.

I am quite happy to discuss the mechanics of the job, for the moment.

She says, I have always thought that they must have souls. When she . . . the woman I work for . . . when she does it there is a noise like cutting a pear . . . but a lot louder. I have helped kill more people than live in this street . . . I counted the houses in the street one night . . . I worked it out.

I say, it is not such a large street . . . a court, not very large.

She says, twice as many as in this street.

I say, but still it is not so many, and we have a problem with population. It is like contraception, if you'll excuse the term, applied a little later.

My voice, I hope, is very calm. It has a certain "professional" touch to it. But my voice gives no indication of what is happening to me. Every single organ in my body is quivering. It is bad. I had wished to take things slowly. There is a slow pleasure to be had from superficial things, then there are more personal things like jobs, the people she likes, where she was born. Only later, much later, should be discussed her fears about the souls of aborted babies. But it is all coming too fast, all becoming too much. I long to touch her clothing. To remove now, so early, an item of clothing, perhaps the shawl, perhaps it would do me no harm to simply remove the shawl.

I stretch my hand, move it along the bed until it is behind her. Just by moving it . . . a fraction . . . just a fraction I can grasp the shawl and pull it slowly away. It falls to the bed, covering my hand.

That was a mistake. A terrible mistake. My hand, already, is searching for the small catch at the back of her pendant. It is difficult. My other hand joins in. The two hands work on the pendant, independent of my will. I am doing what I had planned not to do: rush.

I say, I am old. Soon I will die. It would be nice to make things last.

She says, you are morbid.

She says this as if it were a compliment.

My hands have removed the pendant. I place it on the bed. Now she raises her hands, her two hands, to my face. She says, smell . . .

I sniff. I smell nothing in particular, but then my sense of smell has never been good. While I sniff like some cagey old dog, my hands are busy with the campaign ribbons and plastic flowers which I remove one by one, dropping them to the floor.

She says, what do you smell?

I say, washing up.

She says, it is an antiseptic. I feel I have become soaked in antiseptic, to the marrow of my bones. It has come to upset me.

I say, it would be better if we ceased this discussion for a while, and had some food. We could talk about the food, I have fish fingers again.

She says, I have never told you this but the fish fingers always taste of antiseptic. Everything . . .

I say, you could have told me later, as we progressed. It is not important. It is good that you didn't say, you should not have said, even now, you should have kept it for later.

She says, I'm not hungry, I would rather tell you the truth.

I say, I would rather you didn't.

She says, you know George?

I say, you have mentioned him.

My hands are all of an itch. They have moved to her outermost garment, a peculiar coat, like the coat of a man's suit. I help her out of it and fold it gently.

She says, George and my son . . . you remember.

I say, yes. I remember vaguely, only vaguely . . . if you could refresh my memory.

She says, you are teasing me.

I deny it.

I have started with the next upper garment, a sweater of some description which has a large number 7 on the back. She holds her arms up to make it easier to remove. She says (her voice muffled by the sweater which is now over her head), I made up George, and the son.

I pretend not to hear.

She says, did you hear what I said?

I say, I am not sure.

She says, I made up George and my son . . . they were day-dreams.

I say, you could have kept that for next year. You could have told me at Christmas, it would have been something to look forward to.

She says, how can you look forward to something you don't know is coming?

I say, I know, I knew, that everything was coming, sooner or later, in its own time. I was in no hurry. I have perhaps five years left, it would have filled up the years.

She says, you are talking strangely today.

I say, it has been forced on me.

There is another garment, a blue cardigan, slightly grubby, but still a very pretty blue.

I say, what a beautiful blue.

She says, it is a powder blue.

I say, it is very beautiful, it suits you.

She says, oh, it is not really for me, it belonged to my sister . . . my younger sister.

I say, you never mentioned your younger sister.

She says, you never asked me.

I say, it was intentional.

Now I have all but lost control. The conversation goes on above or below me, somewhere else. I have removed the powder blue cardigan and the red, white, and blue embroidered sweater beneath it. Likewise a blouse which I unfortunately ripped in my haste. I apologized but she only bowed her head meekly.

She says, you have never told me anything about yourself . . . where you work . . .

I am busy with the second blouse, a white silk garment that looks almost new. I say, distractedly, it is as I said, I am unemployed.

She says, but before . . .

I say, I worked for the government for a number of years, a clerk . . .

She says, and before that?

I say, I was at school. It has not been very interesting. There have been few interesting things. Very boring, in fact. What I have had I have eked out, I have made it last, if you understand me, made my few pleasures last. On one occasion I made love to a lady of my acquaintance for thirty-two hours, she was often asleep.

She smiles at me. She says, that sounds . . .

I say, the pity was it was only thirty-two hours, because after that I had to go home, and I had nothing left to do. There was nothing for years after that. It should be possible to do better than thirty-two hours.

She smiles again. I feel I may drown in a million gallons of milk. She says, we can do better than that.

I say, I know, but I had wished it for later. I had wished to save it up for several Christmases from now.

She says, it seems silly . . . to wait.

As I guessed her breasts are large and heavy. I remove the last blouse to reveal them, large and soft with small taut nipples. I transfer my attentions to her skirt, then to a second skirt, and thence to a rather tattered petticoat. Her stockings, I see, are attached to a girdle. I begin to unroll the stocking, unrolling it slowly down the length of her leg. Then the second stocking. And the girdle.

Now she sits, warm and naked, beside me, smiling.

There is only one thing left, an earring on the left ear.

I extend my hand to take it, but she grasps my hand.

She says, leave it.

I say, no.

She says, yes.

I am compelled to use force. I grasp the earring and pull it away. It is not, it would appear, an earring at all, but a zip or catch of some sort. As I pull, her face, then her breasts, peel away. Horrified, I continue to pull, unable to stop until I have stripped her of this unexpected layer.

Standing before me is a male of some twenty odd years. His face is the same as her face, his hair the same. But the breasts have gone, and the hips; they lie in a soft spongy heap on the floor beside the discarded pendant.

She (for I must, from habit, continue to refer to her as "she") seems as surprised as I am. She takes her penis in her hand, curious, kneading it, watching it grow. I watch fascinated. Then I see, on the right ear, a second earring.

I say, excuse me.

She is too preoccupied with the penis to see me reach for the second earring and give it a sharp pull. She sheds another skin, losing, this time, the new-found penis, and revealing, once more, breasts, but smaller and tighter. She is, generally, slimmer, although she was never fat before.

I notice here that she is wearing a suspender belt and stockings. I unroll the first stocking and find the leg is disappearing as I unroll. I have no longer any control over myself. The right leg has disappeared. I begin to unroll the left stocking. The leg, perhaps sensitive to the light, disappears with the rolling.

She sits, legless, on the bed, apparently bemused by the two coats of skin on the floor.

I touch her hair, testing it. A wig. Underneath a bald head.

I take her hand, wishing to reassure her. It removes itself from her body. I am talking to her. Touching her, wishing that she should answer me. But with each touch she is dismembered, slowly, limb by limb. Until, headless, armless, legless, I carelessly lose my grip and she falls to the floor. There is a sharp noise, rather like breaking glass.

Bending down I discover among the fragments a small doll, hairless, eyeless, and white from head to toe.

"Do You Love Me?"

1 The Role of the Cartographers

Perhaps a few words about the role of the Cartographers in our present society are warranted.

To begin with one must understand the nature of the yearly census, a manifestation of our desire to know, always, exactly where we stand. The census, originally a count of the population, has gradually extended until it has become a total inventory of the contents of the nation, a mammoth task which is continuing all the time—no sooner has one census been announced than work on another begins.

The results of the census play an important part in our national life and have, for many years, been the pivot point for the yearly "Festival of the Corn" (an ancient festival, related to the wealth of the earth).

We have a passion for lists. And nowhere is this more clearly illustrated than in the Festival of the Corn which takes place in midsummer, the weather always being fine and warm. On the night of the festival, the householders move their goods and possessions, all furniture, electrical goods, clothing, rugs, kitchen utensils, bathrobes, slippers, cushions, lawnmowers, curtains, doorstops, heirlooms, cameras, and anything else that can be moved into the street so that the census officials may the more easily check the inventory of each household.

The Festival of the Corn is, however, much more than a clerical affair. And, the day over and the night come, the householders invite each other to view their possessions which they refer to, on this night, as gifts. It is like nothing more than a wedding feast—there is much cooking, all sorts of traditional dishes, fine wines, strong liquors, music is played loudly in quiet neighbourhoods, strangers copulate with strangers, men dance together, and maidens in yellow robes distribute small barley sugar corncobs to young and old alike.

And in all this the role of the Cartographers is perhaps the most important, for our people crave, more than anything else, to know the extent of the nation, to know, exactly, the shape of the coastline, to hear what land may have been lost to the sea, to know what has been reclaimed and what is still in doubt. If the Cartographers' report is good the Festival of the Corn will be a good festival. If the report is bad, one can always sense, for all the dancing and drinking, a feeling of nervousness and apprehension in the revellers, a certain desperation. In the year of a bad Cartographers' report there will always be fights and, occasionally, some property will be stolen as citizens attempt to compensate themselves for their sense of loss.

Because of the importance of their job the Cartographers have become an elite—well-paid, admired, envied, and having no small opinion of themselves. It is said by some that they are over-proud, immoral, vain and foot-loose, and it is perhaps the last charge (by necessity true) that brings about the others. For the Cartographers spend their years travelling up and down the coast, along the great rivers, traversing great mountains and vast deserts. They travel in small parties of three, four, sometimes five, making their own time, working as they please, because eventually it is their own responsibility to see that their team's task is completed in time.

My father, a Cartographer himself, often told me stories about himself or his colleagues and the adventures they had in the wilderness.

There were other stories, however, that always remained in my mind and, as a child, caused me considerable anxiety. These were the stories of the nether regions and I doubt if they were known outside a very small circle of Cartographers and government officials. As a child in a house frequented by Cartographers, I often heard these tales which invariably made me cling closely to my mother's skirts.

It appears that for some time certain regions of the country had become less and less real and these regions were regarded fearfully even by the Cartographers, who prided themselves on their courage. The regions in question were invariably uninhabited, unused for agriculture or industry. There were certain sections of the Halverson Ranges, vast stretches of the Greater Desert, and long pieces of coastline which had begun to slowly disappear like the image on an improperly fixed photograph.

It was because of these nebulous areas that the Fischerscope was introduced. The Fischerscope is not unlike radar in its principle and is able to detect the presence of any object, no matter how dematerialized or insubstantial. In this way the Cartographers were still able to map the questionable parts of the nether regions. To have returned with blanks on the maps would have created such public anxiety that no one dared think what it might do to the stability of our society. I now have reason to believe that certain areas of the country disappeared so completely that even the Fischerscope could not detect them and the Cartographers, acting under political pressure, used old maps to fake-in the missing sections. If my theory is grounded in fact, and I am sure it is, it would explain my father's cynicism about the Festival of the Corn.

2 The Archetypal Cartographer

My father was in his fifties but he had kept himself in good shape. His skin was brown and his muscles still firm. He was a tall man with a thick head of grey hair, a slightly less grey moustache and a long aquiline nose. Sitting on a horse he looked as proud and cruel as Genghis Khan. Lying on the beach clad only in bathers and sunglasses he still managed to retain his authoritative air.

Beside him I always felt as if I had betrayed him. I was slightly built, more like my mother.

It was the day before the festival and we lay on the beach, my father, my mother, my girlfriend and I. As was usual in these circumstances my father addressed all his remarks to Karen. He never considered the members of his own family worth talking to. I always had the uncomfortable feeling that he was flirting with my girlfriends and I never knew what to do about it.

People were lying in groups up and down the beach. Near us a family of five were playing with a large beach ball.

"Look at those fools," my father said to Karen.

"Why are they fools?" Karen asked.

"They're fools," said my father. "They were born fools and they'll die fools. Tomorrow they'll dance in the streets and drink too much."

"So." said Karen triumphantly, in the manner of one who has become privy to secret information. "It will be a good Cartographers' report?"

My father roared with laugher.

Karen looked hurt and pouted. "Am I a fool?"

"No," my father said, "you're really quite splendid."

3 The Most Famous Festival

The festival, as it turned out, was the greatest disaster in living memory.

The Cartographers' report was excellent, the weather was fine, but somewhere something had gone wrong.

The news was confusing. The television said that, in spite of the good report, various items had been stolen very early in the night. Later there was a news flash to say that a large house had completely disappeared in Howie Street.

Later still we looked out the window to see a huge band of people carrying lighted torches. There was a lot of shouting. The same image, exactly, was on the television and a reporter was explaining that bands of vigilantes were out looking for thieves.

My father stood at the window, a martini in his hand, and watched the vigilantes set alight a house opposite.

My mother wanted to know what we should do.

"Come and watch the fools," my father said, "they're incredible."

4 The I.C.I. Incident

The next day the I.C.I. building disappeared in front of a crowd of two thousand people. It took two hours. The crowd stood silently as the great steel and glass structure slowly faded before them.

The staff who were evacuated looked pale and shaken. The

caretaker who was amongst the last to leave looked almost translucent. In the days that followed he made some name for himself as a mystic, claiming that he had been able to see other worlds, layer upon layer, through the fabric of the here and now.

5 Behaviour when Confronted with Dematerialization

The anger of our people when confronted with acts of theft has always been legendary and was certainly highlighted by the incidents which occurred on the night of the festival.

But the fury exhibited on this famous night could not compare with the intensity of emotion displayed by those who witnessed the earliest scenes of dematerialization.

The silent crowd who watched the I.C.I. building erupted into hysteria when they realized that it had finally gone and wasn't likely to come back.

It was like some monstrous theft for which punishment must be meted out.

They stormed into the Shell building next door and smashed desks and ripped down office partitions. Reporters who attended the scene were rarely impartial observers, but one of the coolerheaded members of the press remarked on the great number of weeping men and women who hurled typewriters from windows and scattered files through crowds of frightened office workers.

Five days later they displayed similar anger when the Shell building itself disappeared.

6 Behaviour of Those Dematerializing

The first reports of dematerializing people were not generally believed and were suppressed by the media. But these things were soon common knowledge and few families were untouched by them. Such incidents were obviously not all the same but in many victims there was a tendency to exhibit extreme aggression towards those around them. Murders and assaults committed by these unfortunates were not uncommon and in most cases they exhibited an almost unbelievable rage, as if they were the victims of a shocking betrayal.

My friend James Bray was once stopped in the street by a very beautiful woman who clawed and scratched at his face and said: "You did this to me you bastard, you did this to me."

He had never seen her before but he confessed that, in some irrational way, he felt responsible and didn't defend himself. Fortunately she disappeared before she could do him much damage.

7 Some Theories that Arose at the Time

1 The world is merely a dream dreamt by god who is waking after a long sleep. When he is properly awake the world will disappear completely. When the world disappears we will disappear with it and be happy.

2 The world has become sensitive to light. In the same way that prolonged use of say penicillin can suddenly result in a dangerous allergy, prolonged exposure of the world to the sun has made it sensitive to light.

The advocates of this theory could be seen bustling through the city crowds in their long, hooded black robes.

3 The fact that the world is disappearing has been caused by the sloppy work of the Cartographers and census-takers. Those who filled out their census forms incorrectly would lose those items they had neglected to describe. People overlooked in the census by impatient officials would also disappear. A strong pressure group demanded that a new census be taken quickly before matters got worse.

8 My Father's Theory

The world, according to my father, was exactly like the human body and had its own defence mechanisms with which it defended itself against anything that either threatened it or was unnecessary to it. The I.C.I. building and the I.C.I. company had obviously constituted some threat to the world or had simply been irrelevant. That's why it had disappeared and not because some damn fool god was waking up and rubbing his eyes.

"I don't believe in god," my father said. "Humanity is god. Humanity is the only god I know. If humanity doesn't need something it will disappear. People who are not loved will disappear. Everything that is not loved will disappear from the face of the earth. We only exist through the love of others and that's what it's all about."

9 A Contradiction
"Look at those fools," my father said, "they wouldn't know if they were up themselves."

10 An Unpleasant Scene
The world at this time was full of unpleasant and disturbing scenes. One that I recall vividly took place in the middle of the city on a hot, sultry Tuesday afternoon. It was about one-thirty and I was waiting for Karen by the post office when a man of forty or so ran past me. He was dematerializing rapidly. Everybody seemed to be deliberately looking the other way, which seemed to me to make him dematerialize faster. I stared at him hard, hoping that I could do something to keep him there until help arrived. I tried to love him, because I believed in my father's theory. I thought, I must love that man. But his face irritated me. It is not so easy to love a stranger and I'm ashamed to say that he had the small mouth and close-together eyes that I have always disliked in a person. I tried to love him but I'm afraid I failed.

While I watched he tried to hail taxi after taxi. But the taxi drivers were only too well aware of what was happening and had no wish to spend their time driving a passenger who, at any moment, might cease to exist. They looked the other way or put up their NOT FOR HIRE signs.

Finally he managed to waylay a taxi at some traffic lights. By this time he was so insubstantial that I could see right through him. He was beginning to shout. A terrible thin noise, but penetrating none the less. He tried to open the cab door, but the driver had already locked it. I could hear the man's voice, high and piercing: "I want to go home." He repeated it over and over again. "I want to go home to my wife."

The taxi drove off when the lights changed. There was a lull in the traffic. People had fled the corner and left it deserted and it was I alone who saw the man finally disappear.

I felt sick.

Karen arrived five minutes later and found me pale and shaken. "Are you all right?" she said.

"Do you love me?" I said.

11 The Nether Regions

My father had an irritating way of explaining things to me I already understood, refusing to stop no matter how much I said "I know" or "You told me before."

Thus he expounded on the significance of the nether regions, adopting the tone of a lecturer speaking to a class of particularly backward children.

"As you know," he said, "the nether regions were amongst the first to disappear and this in itself is significant. These regions, I'm sure you know, are seldom visited by men and only then by people like me whose sole job is to make sure that they're still there. We had no use for these areas, these deserts, swamps, and coastlines which is why, of course, they disappeared. They were merely possessions of ours and if they had any use at all it was as symbols for our poets, writers and film-makers. They were used as symbols of alienation, lovelessness, loneliness, uselessness and so on. Do you get what I mean?"

"Yes," I said, "I get what you mean."

"But do you?" My father insisted. "But do you really, I wonder." He examined me seriously, musing on the possibilities of my understanding him. "How old are you?"

"Twenty," I said.

"I knew, of course," he said. "Do you understand the significance of the nether regions?"

I sighed, a little too loudly and my father narrowed his eyes. Quickly I said: "They are like everything else. They're like the cities. The cities are deserts where people are alone and lonely. They don't love one another."

"Don't love one another," intoned my father, also sighing. "We no longer love one another. When we realize that we need one another we will stop disappearing. This is a lesson to us. A hard lesson, but, I hope, an effective one."

My father continued to speak, but I watched him without listening. After a few minutes he stopped abruptly: "Are you listening to me?" he said. I was surprised to detect real concern in his voice. He looked at me questioningly. "I've always looked after you," he said, "ever since you were little."

12 The Cartographers' Fall

I don't know when it was that I noticed that my father had become depressed. It probably happened quite gradually without either my mother or me noticing it.

Even when I did become aware of it I attributed it to a woman. My father had a number of lovers and his moods usually reflected the success or failure of these relationships.

But I know now that he had heard already of Hurst and Jamov, the first two Cartographers to disappear. The news was suppressed for several weeks and then, somehow or other, leaked to the press. Certainly the Cartographers had enemies amongst the civil servants who regarded them as over-proud and overpaid, and it was probably from one of these civil servants that the press heard the news.

When the news finally broke I understood my father's depression and felt sorry for him.

I didn't know how to help him. I wanted, badly, to make him happy. I had never ever been able to give him anything or do anything for him that he couldn't do better himself. Now I wanted to help him, to show him I understood.

I found him sitting in front of the television one night when I returned from my office and I sat quietly beside him. He seemed more kindly now and he placed his hand on my knee and patted it.

I sat there for a while, overcome with the new warmth of this relationship and then, unable to contain my emotion any more, I blurted out: "You could change your job."

My father stiffened and sat bolt upright. The pressure of his hand on my knee increased until I yelped with pain, and still he held on, hurting me terribly.

"You are a fool," he said, "you wouldn't know if you were up yourself."

Through the pain in my leg, I felt the intensity of my father's fear.

13 Why the World Needs Cartographers

My father woke me at 3 a.m. to tell me why the world needed Cartographers. He smelled of whisky and seemed, once again, to be very gentle.

"The world needs Cartographers," he said softly, "because if they didn't have Cartographers the fools wouldn't know where they were. They wouldn't know if they were up themselves if they didn't have a Cartographer to tell them what's happening. The world needs Cartographers," my father said, "it fucking well needs Cartographers."

14 One Final Scene

Let me describe a final scene to you: I am sitting on the sofa my father brought home when I was five years old. I am watching television. My father is sitting in a leather armchair that once belonged to his father and which has always been exclusively his. My mother is sitting in the dining alcove with her cards spread across the table, playing one more interminable game of patience.

I glance casually across at my father to see if he is doing anything more than stare into space, and notice, with a terrible shock, that he is showing the first signs of dematerializing.

"What are you staring at?" My father, in fact, has been staring at me.

"Nothing."

"Well, don't."

Nervously I return my eyes to the inanity of the television. I don't know what to do. Should I tell my father that he is dematerializing? If I don't tell him will he notice? I feel I should do something but I can feel, already, the anger in his voice. His anger is nothing new. But this is possibly the beginning of a tide of uncontrollable rage. If he knows he is dematerializing, he will think I don't love him. He will blame me. He will attack me. Old as he is, he is still considerably stronger than I am and he could hurt me badly. I stare determinedly at the television and feel my father's eyes on me.

I try to feel love for my father, I try very, very hard.

I attempt to remember how I felt about him when I was little, in the days when he was still occasionally tender towards me.

But it's no good.

Because I can only remember how he has hit me, hurt me, humiliated me and flirted with my girlfriends. I realize, with a flush of panic and guilt, that I don't love him. In spite of which I say: "I love you."

My mother looks up sharply from her cards and lets out a surprised cry.

I turn to my father. He has almost disappeared. I can see the leather of the chair through his stomach.

I don't know whether it is my unconvincing declaration of love or my mother's exclamation that makes my father laugh. For whatever reason, he begins to laugh uncontrollably: "You bloody fools," he gasps, "I wish you could see the looks on your bloody silly faces."

And then he is gone.

My mother looks across at me nervously, a card still in her hand. "Do you love me?" she asks.

The Chance

1

It was three summers since the Fastalogians had arrived to set up the Genetic Lottery, but it had got so no one gave a damn about what season it was. It was hot. It was steamy. I spent my days in furies and tempers, half-drunk. A six-pack of beer got me to sleep. I didn't have the money for more fanciful drugs and I should have been saving for a Chance. But to save the dollars for a Chance meant six months without grog or any other solace.

There were nights, bitter and lonely, when I felt beyond the Fastalogian alternative, and ready for the other one, to join the Leapers in their suicidal drops from the roofs of buildings and the girders of bridges. I had witnessed a dozen or more. They fell like over-ripe fruit from the rotten trees of a forgotten orchard.

I was overwhelmed by a feeling of great loss. I yearned for lost time, lost childhoods, seasons for Chrissake, the time when peaches are ripe, the time when the river drops after the snow has all melted and it's just low enough to wade and the water freezes your balls and you can walk for miles with little pale crayfish scuttling backwards away from your black-booted feet. Also you can use the dragonfly larva as live bait, casting it out gently and letting it drift downstream to where big old brown trout, their lower jaws grown long and hooked upwards, lie waiting.

The days get hot and clear then and the land is like a tinder box. Old men lighting cigarettes are careful to put the burnt matches back into the matchbox, a habit one sometimes sees carried on into the city by younger people who don't know why they're doing it, messengers carrying notes written in a foreign language.

But all this was once common knowledge, in the days when things were always the same and newness was something as delightful and strange as the little boiled sweets we would be given on Sunday morning.

Those were the days before the Americans came, and before the Fastalogians who succeeded them, descending in their space ships from god knows what unimaginable worlds. And at first we thought them preferable to the Americans. But what the Americans did to us with their yearly car models and two-weekly cigarette lighters was nothing compared to the Fastalogians who introduced concepts so dazzling that we fell prey to them wholesale like South Sea Islanders exposed to the common cold.

The Fastalogians were the universe's bush-mechanics, charlatans, gypsies: raggle-taggle collections of equipment always going wrong. Their Lottery Rooms were always a mess of wires, the floors always littered with dead printed circuits like cigarette ends.

It was difficult to have complete faith in them, yet they could be persuasive enough. Their attitude was eager, frenetic almost, as they attempted to please in the most childish way imaginable. (In confrontation they became much less pleasant, turning curiously evasive while their voices assumed a high-pitched, nasal, wheedling characteristic.)

In appearance they were so much less threatening than the Americans. Their clothes were worn badly, ill-fitting, often with childish mistakes, like buttoning the third button through the fourth buttonhole. They seemed to us to be lonely and puzzled and even while they controlled us we managed to feel a smiling superiority to them. Their music was not the music of an inhuman oppressor. It had surprising fervour, like Hungarian rhapsodies. One was reminded of Bartók, and wondered about the feelings of being so many light years from home.

Their business was the Genetic Lottery or The Chance, whatever you cared to call it. It was, of course, a trick, but we had nothing to question them with. We had only accusations, suspicions, fears that things were not as they were described. If they told us that we could buy a second or third Chance in the Lottery most of us took it, even if we didn't know how it worked, or if it worked the way they said it did.

We were used to not understanding. It had become a habit with the Americans who had left us with a technology we could neither control nor understand. So our failure to grasp the technicalities or even the principles of the Genetic Lottery in no way prevented us from embracing it enthusiastically. After all, we had never grasped the technicalities of the television sets the Americans sold us. Our curiosity about how things worked had atrophied to such an extent that few of us bothered with understanding such things as how the tides worked and why some trees lost their leaves in autumn. It was enough that someone somewhere understood these things. Thus we had no interest in the table of elements that make up all matter, nor in the names of the atomic sub-particles our very bodies were built from. Such was the way we were prepared, like South Sea Islanders, like yearning gnostics waiting to be pointed in the direction of the first tin shed called "God".

So now for two thousand inter-galactic dollars (IG$2,000) we could go in the Lottery and come out with a different age, a different body, a different voice and still carry our memories (allowing for a little leakage) more or less intact.

It proved the last straw. The total embrace of a cancerous philosophy of change. The populace became like mercury in each other's minds and arms. Institutions that had proved the very basis of our society (the family, the neighbourhood, marriage) cracked and split apart in the face of a new shrill current of desperate selfishness. The city itself stood like an external endorsement to this internal collapse and recalled the most exotic places (Calcutta, for instance) where the rich had once journeyed to experience the thrilling stink of poverty, the smell of danger, and the just-contained threat of violence born of envy.

Here also were the signs of fragmentation, of religious confusion, of sects decadent and strict. Wild-haired holymen in loincloths, palm-readers, seers, revolutionaries without followings (the Hups, the Namers, the L.A.K.). Gurus in helicopters flew through the air, whilst bandits roamed the countryside in search of travellers who were no longer intent on adventure and the beauty of nature, but were forced to travel by necessity and who moved in nervous groups, well-armed and thankful to be alive when they returned.

It was an edgy and distrustful group of people that made up our society, motivated by nothing but their self-preservation and their blind belief in their next Chance. To the Fastalogians they were nothing but cattle. Their sole function was to provide a highly favourable inter-galactic balance of payments.

It was through these streets that I strode, muttering, continually on the verge of either anger or tears. I was cut adrift, unconnected. My face in the mirror at morning was not the face that my mind had started living with. It was a battered, red, broken-nosed face, marked by great quizzical eyebrows, intense black eyes, and tangled wiry hair. I had been through the lottery and lost. I had got myself the body of an ageing street-fighter. It was a body built to contain furies. It suited me. The arrogant Gurus and the ugly Hups stepped aside when I stormed down their streets on my daily course between the boarding house where I lived to the Department of Parks where I was employed as a gardener. I didn't work much. I played cards with the others. the botanical gardens were slowly being choked by "Burning Glory", a prickly crimson flowering bush the Fastalogians had imported either by accident or design. It was our job to remove it. Instead, we used it as cover for our cheating card games. Behind its red blazing hedges we lied and fought and, on occasion, fornicated. We were not a pretty sight.

It was from here that I walked back to the boarding house with my beer under my arm, and it was on a Tuesday afternoon that I saw her, just beyond the gardens and a block down from the Chance Centre in Grove Street. She was sitting on the footpath with a body beside her, an old man, his hair white and wispy, his face brown and wrinkled like a walnut. He was dressed very formally in a three-piece grey suit and had an old-fashioned watch chain across the waistcoat. I assumed that the corpse was her grandfather. Since the puppet government had dropped its funeral assistance plan this was how poor people raised money for funerals. It was a common sight to see dead bodies in rented suits being displayed on the footpaths. So it was not the old man who attracted my attention but the young woman who sat beside him.

"Money," she said, "Money for an old man to lie in peace."

I stopped willingly. She had her dark hair cut quite short and

58

rather badly. Her eyebrows were full, but perfectly arched, her features were saved from being too regular by a mouth that was wider than average. She wore a khaki shirt, a navy blue jacket, filthy trousers and a small gold earring in her right ear.

"I've only got beer," I said, "I've spent all my money on beer."

She grinned a broad and beautiful grin which illuminated her face and made me echo it.

"I'd settle for a beer." And I was surprised to hear shyness.

I sat down on the footpath and we opened the six-pack. Am I being sentimental when I say I shared my beer without calculation? That I sought nothing? It seems unlikely for I had some grasping habits as you'll see soon enough. But I remember nothing of the sort, only that I liked the way she opened the beer bottle. Her hands were large, a bit messed-up. She hooked a broken-nailed finger into the ring-pull and had it off without even looking at what she was doing.

She took a big swallow, wiped her mouth with the back of her hand and said: "Shit, I needed that."

I muttered something about her grandfather, trying to make polite conversation, I was out of the habit.

She shrugged and put the cold bottle on her cheek. "I got him from the morgue."

I didn't understand.

"I bought him for three IGs." She grinned, tapping her head with her middle finger. "Best investment I've ever made."

It was this, more than anything, that got me. I admired cunning in those days, smart moves, cards off the bottom of the deck, anything that tricked the bastards—and "the bastards" were everyone who wasn't me.

So I laughed. A loud deep joyful laugh that made passers-by stare at me. I gave them the fingers-up and they looked away.

She sat on her hands, rocking back and forth on them as she spoke. She had a pleasantly nasal, idiosyncratic voice, slangy and relaxed. "They really go for white hair and tanned faces." She nodded towards a paint tin full of coins and notes. "It's pathetic isn't it? I wouldn't have gotten half this much for my real grandfather. He's too dark. Also, they don't like women much. Men do much better than women."

She had the slightly exaggerated toughness of the very young. I wondered if she'd taken a Chance. It didn't look like it.

We sat and drank the beer. It started to get dark. She lit a mosquito coil and we stayed there in the gloom till we drank the whole lot.

When the last bottle was gone, the small talk that had sustained us went away and left us in an uneasy area of silence. Now suspicion hit me with its fire-hot pinpricks. I had been conned for my beer. I would go home and lie awake without its benefits. It would be a hot sleepless night and I would curse myself for my gullibility. I, who was shrewd and untrickable, had been tricked.

But she stood and stretched and said, "Come on, now I've drunk your beer, I'll buy you a meal."

We walked away and left the body for whoever wanted it. I never saw the old man again.

The next day he was gone.

2

I cannot explain what it was like to sit in a restaurant with a woman. I felt embarrassed, awkward, and so pleased that I couldn't put one foot straight in front of the other.

I fancy I was graciously old-fashioned.

I pulled out her chair for her, I remember, and saw the look she shot me, both pleased and alarmed. It was a shocked, fast flick of the eyes. Possibly she sensed the powerful fantasies that lonely men create, steel columns of passion appended with leather straps and tiny mirrors.

It was nearly a year since I'd talked to a woman, and that one stole my money and even managed to lift two blankets from my sleeping body. Twelve dull stupid drugged and drunken months had passed, dissolving from the dregs of one day into the sink of the next.

The restaurant was one of those Fasta Cafeterias that had sprung up, noisy, messy, with harsh lighting and long rows of bright white tables that were never ever filled. The service was bad and in the end we went to the kitchen where we helped ourselves from the long trays of food, Fastalogian salads with their dried intoxicating mushrooms, and that strange milky pap they are so fond of. She piled her plate high with everything and I envied the calm that allowed her such an appetite. On any other night I would have done the same, guzzling and gorging myself on my free meal.

Finally, tripping over each other, we returned to our table. She bought two more beers and I thanked her for that silently.

Here I was. With a woman. Like real people.

I smiled broadly at the thought. She caught me and was, I think, pleased to have something to hang on to. So we got hold of that smile and wrung it for all it was worth.

Being desperate, impatient, I told her the truth about the smile. The directness was pleasing to her. I watched how she leant into my words without fear or reservation, displaying none of the shiftiness that danced through most social intercourse in those days. But I was as calculating and cunning as only the very lonely learn how to be. Estimating her interest, I selected the things which would be most pleasing for her. I steered the course of what I told, telling her things about me which fascinated her most. She was pleased by my confessions. I gave her many. She was strong and young and confident. She couldn't see my deviousness and, no matter what I told her of loneliness, she couldn't taste the stale self-hating afternoons or suspect the callousness they engendered.

And I bathed in her beauty, delighting in the confidence it brought her, the certainty of small mannerisms, the chop of that beautiful rough-fingered hand when making a point. But also, this: the tentative question marks she hooked on to the ends of her most definite assertions. So I was impressed by her strength and charmed by her vulnerability all at once.

One could not have asked for more.

And this also I confessed to her, for it pleased her to be talked about and it gave me an intoxicating pleasure to be on such intimate terms.

And I confessed why I had confessed.

My conversation was mirrors within mirrors, onion skin behind onion skin. I revealed motives behind motives. I was amazing. I felt myself to be both saint and pirate, as beautiful and gnarled as an ancient olive. I talked with intensity. I devoured her, not like some poor beggar (which I was) but like a prince, a stylish master of the most elegant dissertations.

She ate ravenously, but in no way neglected to listen. She talked impulsively with her mouth full. With mushrooms dropping from her mouth, she made a point. It made her beautiful, not ugly.

I have always enjoyed women who, whilst being conventionally feminine enough in their appearance, have exhibited certain behavioural traits more commonly associated with men. A bare-breasted women working on a tractor is the fastest, crudest approximation I can provide. An image, incidentally, guaranteed to give me an aching erection, which it has, on many lonely nights.

But to come back to my new friend who rolled a cigarette with hands which might have been the hands of an apprentice bricklayer, hands which were connected to breasts which were connected to other parts doubtless female in gender, who had such grace and beauty in her form and manner and yet had had her hair shorn in such a manner as to deny her beauty.

She was tall, my height. Across the table I noted that her hands were as large as mine. They matched. The excitement was exquisite. I anticipated nothing, vibrating in the crystal of the moment.

We talked, finally, as everyone must, about the Lottery, for the Lottery was life in those days and all of us, or most of us, were saving for another Chance.

"I'm taking a Chance next week," she said.

"Good luck," I said. It was automatic. That's how life had got.

"You look like you haven't."

"Thank you," I said. It was a compliment, like saying that my shirt suited me. "But I've had four."

"You move nicely," she smiled. "I was watching you in the kitchen. You're not awkward at all."

"You move nicely too," I grinned. "I was watching you too. You're crazy to take a Chance, what do you want?"

"A people's body." She said it fast, briskly, and stared at me challengingly.

"A what?"

"A people's body." She picked up a knife, examined it and put it down.

It dawned on me. "Oh, you're a Hup."

Thinking back, I'm surprised I knew anything about the Hups. They were one of a hundred or more revolutionary crackpots. I didn't give a damn about politics and I thought every little group was more insane than the next.

And here, goddamn it, I was having dinner with a Hup, a rich crazy who thought the way to fight the revolution was to have a body as grotesque and ill-formed as my friends at the Parks and Gardens.

"My parents took the Chance last week."

"How did it go?"

"I didn't see them. They've gone to . . ." she hesitated ". . . to another place where they're needed." She had become quiet now, and serious, explaining that her parents had upper-class bodies like hers, that their ideas were not at home with their physiognomy (a word I had to ask her to explain), that they would form the revolutionary vanguard to lead the misshapen Lumpen Proletariat (another term I'd never heard before) to overthrow the Fastas and their puppets.

I had a desperate desire to change the subject, to plug my ears, to shut my eyes. I wouldn't have been any different if I'd discovered she was a mystic or a follower of Hiwi Kaj.

"Anyway," I said, "you've got a beautiful body."

"Why did you say that?"

I could have said that I'd spent enough of my life with her beloved Lumpen Proletariat to hold them in no great esteem, that the very reason I was enjoying her company so much was because she was so unlike them. But I didn't want to pursue it. I shrugged, grinned stupidly, and filled her glass with beer.

Her eyes flashed at my shrug. I don't know why people say "flashed", but I swear there was red in her eyes. She looked hurt, stung, and ready to attack.

She withdrew from me, leaning back in her chair and folding her arms. "What do you think is beautiful?"

Before I could answer she was leaning back into the table, but this time her voice was louder.

"What is more beautiful, a parrot or a crow?"

"A parrot, if you mean a rosella. But I don't know much about parrots."

"What's wrong with a crow?"

"A crow is black and awkward-looking. It's heavy. Its cry is unattractive."

"What makes its cry unattractive?"

I was sick of the game, and exhausted with such sudden mental exercise.

"It sounds forlorn," I offered.

"Do you think that it is the crow's intention, to sound forlorn? Perhaps you are merely ignorant and don't know how to listen to a crow."

"Certainly, I'm ignorant." It was true, of course, but the observation stung a little. I was very aware of my ignorance in those days. I felt it keenly.

"If you could kill a parrot or a crow which would you kill?"

"Why would I want to kill either of them?"

"But if you had to, for whatever reason."

"The crow, I suppose. Or possibly the parrot. Whichever was the smallest."

Her eyes were alight and fierce. She rolled a cigarette without looking at it. Her face suddenly looked extraordinarily beautiful, her eyes glistening with emotion, the colour high in her cheeks, a peculiar half-smile on her wide mouth.

"Which breasts are best?"

I laughed. "I don't know."

"Which legs?"

"I don't know. I like long legs."

"Like the film stars."

Like yours, I thought. "Yes."

"Is that really your idea of beautiful?"

She was angry with me now, had decided to call me enemy. I did not feel enemy and didn't want to be. My mind felt fat and flabby, unused, numb. I forgot my irritation with her ideas. I set all that aside. In the world of ideas I had no principles. An idea was of no worth to me, not worth fighting for. I would fight for a beer, a meal, a woman, but never an idea.

"I like grevilleas," I said greasily.

She looked blank. I thought as much! "Which are they?" I had her at a loss.

"They're small bushes. They grow in clay, in the harshest situations. Around rocks, on dry hillsides. If you come fishing with me, I'll show you. The leaves are more like spikes. They look dull and harsh. No one would think to look at them twice. But in November," I smiled, "they have flowers like glorious red spiders. I think they're beautiful."

"But in October?"

"In October I know what they'll be like in November."

She smiled. She must have wanted to like me. I was disgusted with my argument. It had been cloying and saccharine even to me. I hadn't been quite sure what to say, but it seems I hit the nail on the head.

"Does it hurt?" she asked suddenly.

"What?"

"The Chance. Is it painful, or is it like they say?"

"It makes you vomit a lot, and feel ill, but it doesn't hurt. It's more a difficult time for your head."

She drained her beer and began to grin at me. "I was just thinking," she said.

"Thinking what?"

"I was thinking that if you have anything more to do with me it'll be a hard time for your head too."

I looked at her grinning face, disbelievingly.

I found out later that she hadn't been joking.

3

To cut a long and predictable story short, we got on well together, if you'll allow for the odd lie on my part and what must have been more than a considerable suppression of commonsense on hers.

I left my outcast acquaintances behind to fight and steal, and occasionally murder each other in the boarding house. I returned there only to pick up my fishing rod. I took it round to her place at Pier Street swaggering like a sailor on leave. I was in a flamboyant, extravagant mood and left behind my other ratty possessions. They didn't fit my new situation.

Thus, to the joys of living with an eccentric and beautiful woman I added the even more novel experience of a home. Either one of these changes would have brought me some measure of contentment, but the combination of the two of them was almost too good to be true.

I was in no way prepared for them. I had been too long a grabber, a survivor.

So when I say that I became obsessed with hanging on to these things, using every shred of guile I had learned in my old life, do not judge me harshly. The world was not the way it is now. It was a bitter jungle of a place, worse, because even in the jungle there is co-operation, altruism, community.

Regarding the events that followed I feel neither pride nor shame. Regret, certainly, but regret is a useless emotion. I was ignorant, short-sighted, bigoted, but in my situation it is inconceivable that I could have been anything else.

But now let me describe for you Carla's home as I came to know it, not as I saw it at first, for then I only felt the warmth of old timbers and delighted in the dozens of small signs of domesticity everywhere about me: a toothbrush in a glass, dirty clothes overflowing from a blue cane laundry basket, a made bed, dishes draining in a sink, books, papers, letters from friends, all the trappings of a life I had long abandoned, many Chances ago.

The house had once been a warehouse, long before the time of the Americans. It was clad with unpainted boards that had turned a gentle silver, ageing with a grace that one rarely saw in those days.

One ascended the stairs from the Pier Street wharf itself. A wooden door. A large key. Inside: a floor of grooved boards, dark with age.

The walls showed their bones: timber joists and beams, roughly nailed in the old style, but solid as a rock.

High in the ceiling was a sleeping platform, below it a simple kitchen filled with minor miracles: a hot water tap, a stove, a refrigerator, saucepans, spices, even a recipe book or two.

The rest of the area was a sitting room, the pride of place being given to three beautiful antique armchairs in the Danish style, their carved arms showing that patina which only age can give.

Add a rusty-coloured old rug, pile books high from the floor, pin Hup posters here and there, and you have it.

Or almost have it, because should you open the old high sliding door (pushing hard, because its rollers are stiff and rusty from the salty air) and the room is full of the sea, the once-great harbour, its waters rarely perturbed by craft, its shoreline dotted with rusting hulks of forgotten ships, great tankers from the oil age, tugs, and ferries which, even a year before, had maintained their services in the face of neglect and disinterest on all sides.

Two other doors led off the main room: one to a rickety toilet which hung out precariously over the water, the other to a bedroom, its walls stacked with files, books, loose papers, its great bed draped in mosquito netting, for there was no wiring for the customary sonic mosquito repellents and the mosquitoes carried Fasta Fever with the same dedicated enthusiasm that others of their family had once carried malaria.

The place revealed its secrets fast enough, but Carla, of course, did not divulge hers quite so readily. Frankly, it suited me. I was happy to see what I was shown and never worried about what was hidden away.

I mentioned nothing of Hups or revolution and she, for her part, seemed to have forgotten the matter. My assumption (arrogantly made) was that she would put off her Chance indefinitely. People rarely plunged into the rigours of the Lottery when they were happy with their life. I was delighted with mine, and I assumed she was with hers.

I had never known anyone like her. She sang beautifully and played the cello with what seemed to me to be real accomplishment. She came to the Park and Gardens and beat us all at poker. To see her walk across to our bed, moving with the easy gait of an Islander, filled me with astonishment and wonder.

I couldn't believe my luck.

She had been born rich but chose to live poor, an idea that was beyond my experience or comprehension. She had read more books in the last year than I had in my life. And when my efforts to hide my ignorance finally gave way in tatters she took to my education with the same enthusiasm she brought to our bed.

Her methods were erratic, to say the least. For each new book she gave me revealed a hundred gaps in my knowledge that would have to be plugged with other books.

I was deluged with the whole artillery of Hup literature: long and difficult works like Gibson's *Class and Genetics*, Schumacher's *Comparative Physiognomy*, Hale's *Wolf Children*.

I didn't care what they were about. If they had been treatises on the history of Rome or the Fasta economic system I would have read them with as much enthusiasm and probably learnt just as little.

Sitting on the wharf I sang her "Rosie Allan's Outlaw Friend", the story of an ill-lettered cattle thief and his love for a young school-mistress. My body was like an old guitar, fine and mellow with beautiful resonance.

The first star appeared.

"The first star," I said.

"It's a planet," she said.

"What's the difference?" I asked.

She produced a school book on the known solar system at breakfast the next morning.

"How in the hell to you know so little?" she said, eating the omelette I'd cooked her.

I stared at the extraordinary rings of Saturn, knowing I'd known some of these things long ago. They brought to mind classrooms on summer days, dust, the smell of oranges, lecture theatres full of formally dressed students with eager faces.

"I guess I just forgot," I said. "Maybe half my memory is walking around in other bodies. And how in the fuck is it that you don't know how to make a decent omelette?"

"I guess," she grinned, "that I just forgot."

She wandered off towards the kitchen with her empty plate but got distracted by an old newspaper she found on the way. She put the plate on the floor and went on to the kitchen where she read the paper, leaning back against the sink.

"You have rich habits," I accused her.

She looked up, arching her eyebrows questioningly.

"You put things down for other people to pick up."

She flushed and spent five minutes picking up things and putting them in unexpected places.

She never mastered the business of tidying up and finally I was the one who became housekeeper.

When the landlord arrived one morning to collect the rent she introduced me as "my house-proud lover". I gave the bastard my street-fighter's sneer and he swallowed the smirk he was starting to grow on his weak little face.

I was the one who opened the doors to the harbour. I swept the floor, I tidied the books and washed the plates. I threw out the old newspapers and took down the posters for Hup meetings and demonstrations which had long since passed.

She came in from work after my first big clean-up and started pulling books out and throwing them on the floor.

"What in the fuck are you doing?"

"Where did you put them?"

"Put what?"

She pulled down a pile of old pamphlets and threw them on the floor as she looked between each one.

"What?"

"My posters, you bastard. How dare you."

I was nonplussed. My view of posters was purely practical. It had never occurred to me that they might have any function other than to advertise what they appeared to advertise. When the event was past the poster had no function.

Confused and angry at her behaviour, I retrieved the posters from the bin in the kitchen.

"You creased them."

"I'm sorry."

She started putting them up again.

"Why did you take them down? It's your house now, is it? Would you like to paint the walls, eh? Do you want to change the furniture, too? Is there anything else that isn't to your liking?"

"Carla," I said, "I'm sorry. I took them down because they were out-of-date."

"Out-of-date," she snorted. "You mean you think they're ugly."

I looked at the poster she was holding, a glorification of crooked forms and ugly faces.

"Well if you want to put it like that, yes, I think they're fucking ugly."

She glowered at me, self-righteous and prim. "You only say

that because you're so conditioned that you can only admire looks like mine. How pathetic. That's why you like me, isn't it?"

Her face was red, the skin taut with rage.

"Isn't it?"

I'd thought this damn Hup thing had gone away, but here it was. The stupidity of it. It drove me insane. Her books became weapons in my hands. I threw them at her, hard, in a frenzy.

"Idiot. Dolt. You don't believe what you say. You're too young to know anything. You don't know what these damn people are like," I poked at the posters, "you're too young to know anything. You're a fool. You're playing with life." I hurled another book. "Playing with it."

She was young and nimble with a boxer's reflexes. She dodged the books easily enough and retaliated viciously, slamming a thick sociology text into the side of my head.

Staggering back to the window I was confronted with the vision of an old man's face, looking in.

I pulled up the window and transferred my abuse in that direction.

"Who in the fuck are you?"

A very nervous old man stood on a long ladder, teetering nervously above the street.

"I'm a painter."

"Well piss off."

He looked down into the street below as I grabbed the top rung of the ladder and gave it a little bit of a shake.

"Who is it?" Carla called.

"It's a painter."

"What's he doing?"

I looked outside. "He's painting the bloody place orange."

The painter, seeing me occupied with other matters, started to retreat down the ladder.

"Hey," I shook the ladder to make him stop.

"It's only a primer," he pleaded.

"It doesn't need any primer," I yelled, "those bloody boards will last a hundred years."

"You're yelling at the wrong person, fellah." The painter was at the bottom of the ladder now, and all the bolder because of it.

"If you touch that ladder again I'll have the civil police here." He backed into the street and shook his finger at me. "They'll do you, my friend, so just watch it."

I slammed the window shut and locked it for good measure. "You've got to talk to the landlord," I said, "before they ruin the place."

"Got to?"

"Please."

Her face became quiet and secretive. She started picking up books and pamphlets and stacking them against the wall with exaggerated care.

"Please Carla."

"You tell them," she shrugged. "I won't be here." She fetched the heavy sociology text from beneath the window and frowned over the bookshelves, looking for a place to put it.

"What in the hell does that mean?"

"It means I'm a Hup. I told you that before. I told you the first time I met you. I'm taking a Chance and you won't like what comes out. I told you before," she repeated, "you've known all along."

"Be buggered you're taking a Chance."

She shrugged. She refused to look at me. She started picking up books and carrying them to the kitchen, her movements uncharacteristically brisk.

"People only take a Chance when they're pissed off. Are you?"

She stood by the stove, the books cradled in her arms, tears streaming down her face.

Even as I held her, even as I stroked her hair, I began to plot to keep her in the body she was born in. It became my obsession.

4

I came home the next night to find the outside of the house bright orange and the inside filled with a collection of people as romantically ugly as any I had ever seen. They betrayed their upper-class origins by dressing their crooked forms in such romantic styles that they were in danger of creating a new foppishness. Faults and infirmities were displayed with a pride that would have been alien to any but a Hup.

A dwarf reclined in a Danish-style armchair, an attenuated hand waving a cigarette. His overalls, obviously tailored, were very soft, an expensive material splattered with "original" paint. If he hadn't been smoking so languorously he might have passed for real.

Next to him, propped against the wall, was the one I later knew as Daniel. The grotesque pock-marks on his face proudly accentuated by the subtle use of make-up and, I swear to God, colour co-ordinated with a flamboyant pink scarf.

Then, a tall thin woman with the most pronounced curvature of the spine and a gaunt face dominated by a most extraordinary hooked nose. Her form was clad in the tightest garments and from it emanated the not unsubtle aroma of power and privilege.

If I had seen them anywhere else I would have found them laughable, not worthy of serious attention. Masters amusing themselves by dressing as servants. Returned tourists clad in beggars' rags. Educated fops doing a bad charade of my tough, grisly companions in the boarding house.

But I was not anywhere else. This was our home and they had turned it into some spiderweb or nightmare where dog turds smell like French wine and roses stink of the charnel-house.

And there squatting in their midst, my most beautiful Carla, her eyes shining with enthusiasm and admiration whilst the hook-nosed lady waved her bony fingers.

I stayed by the door and Carla, smiling too eagerly, came to greet me and introduce me to her friends. I watched her dark eyes flick nervously from one face to the next, fearful of everybody's reaction to me, and mine to them.

I stood awkwardly behind the dwarf as he passed around his snap-shots, photographs taken of him before his Chance.

"Not bad, eh?" he said, showing me a shot of a handsome man on the beach at Cannes. "I was a handsome fellow, eh?"

It was a joke, but I was confused about its meaning. I nodded, embarrassed. The photograph was creased with lines like the palm of an old man's hand.

I looked at the woman's curved back and the gaunt face, trying to find beauty there, imagining holding her in my arms.

She caught my eyes and smiled. "Well young man, what wil!

you do while we have our little meeting?"

God knows what expression crossed my face, but it would have been a mere ripple on the surface of the feelings that boiled within me.

Carla was at my side in an instant, whispering in my ear that it was an important meeting and wouldn't take long. The hook-nosed woman, she said, had an unfortunate manner, was always upsetting everyone, but had, just the same, a heart of gold.

I took my time in leaving, fussing around the room looking for my beautiful light fishing rod with its perfectly preserved old Mitchell reel. I enjoyed the silence while I fossicked around behind books, under chairs, finally discovering it where I knew it was all the time.

In the kitchen, I slapped some bait together, mixing mince meat, flour and garlic, taking my time with this too, forcing them to indulge in awkward small talk about the price of printing and the guru in the electric cape, one of the city's recent contributions to a more picturesque life.

Outside the painters were washing their brushes, having covered half of the bright orange with a pale blue.

The sun was sinking below the broken columns of the Hinden Bridge as I cast into the harbour. I used no sinker, just a teardrop of mince meat, flour and garlic, an enticing meal for a bream.

The water shimmered, pearlescent. The bream attacked, sending sharp signals up the delicate light line. They fought like the fury and showed themselves in flashes of frantic silver. Luderick also swam below my feet, feeding on long ribbons of green weed. A small pink cloud drifted absent-mindedly through a series of metamorphoses. An old work boat passed sitting low in the water like a dumpy brown duck, full of respectability and regular intent.

Yet I was anaesthetized and felt none of what I saw.

For above my head in a garish building slashed with orange and blue I imagined the Hups concluding plans to take Carla away from me.

The water became black with a dark blue wave. The waving reflection of a yellow-lighted window floated at my feet and I heard the high-pitched wheedling laugh of a Fasta in the house above. It was the laugh of a Fasta doing business.

That night I caught ten bream. I killed only two. The others I returned to the melancholy window floating at my feet.

5

The tissues lay beneath the bed. Dead white butterflies, wet with tears and sperm.

The mosquito net, like a giant parody of a wedding veil, hung over us, its fibres luminescent, shimmering with light from the open door.

Carla's head rested on my shoulder, her hair wet from both our tears.

"You could put it off," I whispered. "Another week."

"I can't. You know I can't. If I don't do it when it's booked I'll have to wait six months."

"Then wait . . ."

"I can't."

"We're good together."

"I know."

"It'll get better."

"I know."

"It won't last, if you do it."

"It might, if we try."

I damned the Hups in silence. I cursed them for their warped ideals. If only they could see how ridiculous they looked.

I stroked her brown arm, soothing her in advance of what I said. "It's not right. Your friends haven't become working class. They have a manner. They look disgusting."

She withdrew from me, sitting up to light a cigarette with an angry flourish.

"Ah, you see," she pointed the cigarette at me. "Disgusting. They look disgusting."

"They look like rich fops amusing themselves. They're not real. They look evil."

She slipped out from under the net and began searching through the tangled clothes on the floor, separating hers from mine. "I can't stand this," she said, "I can't stay here."

"You think it's so fucking great to look like the dwarf?" I

screamed. "Would you fuck him? Would you wrap your legs around him? Would you?"

She stood outside the net, very still and very angry. "That's my business."

I was chilled. I hadn't meant it. I hadn't thought it possible. I was trying to make a point. I hadn't believed.

"Did you?" I hated the shrill tone that crept into my voice. I was a child, jealous, hurt.

I jumped out of the bed and started looking for my own clothes. She had my trousers in her hand. I tore them from her.

"I wish you'd just shut-up," I hissed, although she had said nothing. "And don't patronize me with your stupid smart-talk." I was shaking with rage.

She looked me straight in the eye before she punched me.

I laid one straight back.

"That's why I love you, damn you."

"Why?" she screamed, holding her hand over her face. "For God's sake, why?"

"Because we'll both have black eyes."

She started laughing just as I began to cry.

6

I started to write a diary and then stopped. The only page in it says this:

"Saturday. This morning I know that I am in love. I spend the day thinking about her. When I see her in the street she is like a painting that is even better than you remembered. Today we wrestled. She told me she could wrestle me. Who would believe it? What a miracle she is. Ten days to go. I've got to work out something."

7

Wednesday. Meeting day for the freaks.

On the way home I bought a small bag of mushrooms to calm me down a little bit. I walked to Pier Street the slow way, nibbling as I went.

I came through the door ready to face the whole menagerie but they weren't there, only the hook-nosed lady, arranged in tight brown rags and draped across a chair, her bowed legs dangling, one shoe swinging from her toe.

She smiled at me, revealing an uneven line of stained and broken teeth.

"Ah, the famous Lumpy."

"My name is Paul."

She swung her shoe a little too much. It fell to the floor, revealing her mutant toes in all their glory.

"Forgive me. Lumpy is a pet name?" She wiggled her toes. "Something private?"

I ignored her and went to the kitchen to make bait in readiness for my exile on the pier. The damn mince was frozen solid. Carla had tidied it up and put it in the freezer. I dropped it in hot water to thaw it.

"Your mince is frozen."

"Obviously."

She patted the chair next to her with a bony hand.

"Come and sit. We can talk."

"About what?" I disconnected the little Mitchell reel from the rod and started oiling it, first taking off the spool and rinsing the sand from it.

"About life," she waved her hand airily, taking in the room as if it were the entire solar system. "About . . . love. What . . . ever." Her speech had that curious unsure quality common in those who had taken too many Chances, the words spluttered and trickled from her mouth like water from a kinked and tangled garden hose. "You can't go until your mince . . . mince has thawed." She giggled. "You're stuck with me."

I smiled in spite of myself.

"I could always use weed and go after the luderick."

"But the tide is high and the weed will be . . . impossible to get. Sit down." She patted the chair again.

I brought the reel with me and sat next to her slowly dismantling it and laying the parts on the low table. The mushrooms were beginning to work, coating a smooth creamy layer over the gritty irritations in my mind.

"You're upset," she said. I was surprised to hear concern in her voice. I suppressed a desire to look up and see if her features had changed. Her form upset me as much as the soft rotting faces of the beggars who had been stupid enough to make love with the Fastas. So I screwed the little ratchet back in and wiped it twice with oil.

"You shouldn't be upset."

I said nothing, feeling warm and absent-minded, experiencing that slight ringing in the ears you get from eating mushrooms on an empty stomach. I put the spool back on and tightened the tension knob. I was running out of things to do that might give me an excuse not to look at her.

She was close to me. Had she been that close to me when I sat down? In the corner of my eye I could see her gaunt bowed leg, an inch or two from mine. My thick muscled forearm seemed to belong to a different planet, to have been bred for different purposes, to serve sane and sensible ends, to hold children on my knee, to build houses, to fetch and carry the ordinary things of life.

"You shouldn't be upset. You don't have to lose Carla. She loves you. You may find that it is not so bad . . . making love . . . with a Hup." She paused. "You've been eating mushrooms, haven't you?"

The hand patted my knee. "Maybe that's not such a bad thing."

What did she mean? I meant to ask, but forgot I was feeling the hand. I thought of rainbow trout in the clear waters at Dobson's Creek, their brains humming with creamy music while my magnified white hands rubbed their underbellies, tickling them gently before grabbing them, like stolen jewels, and lifting them triumphant in the sunlight. I smelt the heady smell of wild blackberries and the damp fecund odours of rotting wood and bracken.

"We don't forget how to make love when we change."

The later afternoon sun streamed through a high window. The room was golden. On Dobson's Creek there is a shallow run from a deep pool, difficult to work because of overhanging willows, caddis flies hover above the water in the evening light.

The hand on my knee was soft and caressing. Once, many Chances ago, I had my hair cut by a strange old man. He combed so slowly, cut so delicately, my head and my neck were suffused with pleasure. It was in a classroom. Outside someone hit a tennis ball against a brick wall. There were cicadas, I remember, and a water sprinkler threw beads of light on to glistening grass, freshly mown. He cut my hair shorter and shorter till my fingers tingled.

It has been said that the penis has no sense of right or wrong, that it acts with the brainless instinct of a venus fly-trap, but that is not true. It's too easy a reason for the stiffening cock that rose, stretching blindly towards the bony fingers.

"I could show," said the voice, "that it is something quite extraordinary . . . not worse . . . better . . . better . . . better by far, you have nothing to fear."

I knew, I knew exactly in the depth of my clouded mind, what was happening. I didn't resist it. I didn't want to resist it. My purpose was as hers. My reasons probably identical.

Softly, sonorously she recited:

"Which trees are beautiful?

All trees that grow.

Which bird is fairest?"

A zipper undone, my balls held gently, a finger stroked the length of my cock. My eyes shut, questions and queries banished to dusty places.

"The bird that flies.

Which face is fairest?

The faces of the friends of the people of the earth."

A hand, flat-palmed on my rough face, the muscles in my shoulders gently massaged, a finger circling the lips of my anal sphincter.

"Which forms are foul?

The forms of the owners.

The forms of the exploiters.

The forms of the friends of the Fastas."

Legs across my lap, she straddled me. "I will give you a taste . . . just a taste . . . you won't stop Carla . . . you can't stop her."

She moved too fast, her legs gripped mine too hard, the hand on my cock was tugging towards her cunt too hard.

My open eyes stared into her face. The face so foul, so mis-shapen, broken, the skin marked with ruptured capillaries, the green eyes wide, askance, alight with premature triumph.

Drunk on wine I have fucked monstrously ugly whores. Deranged on drugs, blind, insensible, I have grunted like a dog above those whom I would as soon have slaughtered.

But this, no. No, no, no. For whatever reason, no. Even as I stood, shaking and trembling, she clung to me, smiling, not understanding. "Carla will be beautiful. You will do things you never did."

Her grip was strong. I fought through mosquito nets of mushroom haze, layer upon layer that ripped like dusty lace curtains, my arms, flailing, my panic mounting. I had woken underwater, drowning.

I wrenched her hand from my shoulder and she shrieked with pain. I pulled her leg from my waist and she fell back on to the floor, grunting as the wind was knocked from her.

I stood above her, shaking, my heart beating wildly, the head of my cock protruding foolishly from my unzipped trousers, looking as pale and silly as a toadstool.

She struggled to her feet, rearranging her elegant rags and cursing. "You are an ignorant fool. You are a stupid, ignorant, reactionary fool. You have breathed the Fastas' lies for so long that your rotten body is soaked with them. You stink of lies . . . do you . . . know who I am?"

I stared at her, panting.

"I am Jane Larange."

For a second I couldn't remember who Jane Larange was, then it came to me:"The actress?" The once beautiful and famous.

I shook my head. "You silly bugger. What in God's name have you done to yourself?"

She went to her handbag, looking for a cigarette. "We will kill the Fastas," she said, smiling at me, "and we will kill their puppets and their leeches."

She stalked to the kitchen and lifted the mince meat from the sink. "Your mince is thawed."

The mince was pale and wet. It took more flour than usual to get it to the right consistency. She watched me, leaning against the sink, smoking her perfumed cigarette.

"Look at you, puddling around with stinking meat like a child playing with shit. You would rather play with shit than act like a responsible adult. When the adults come you will slink off and kill fish." She gave a grunt. "Poor Carla."

"Poor Carla." She made me laugh. "You try and fuck me and then you say 'poor Carla'!"

"You are not only ugly," she said, "you are also stupid. I did that for Carla. Do you imagine I like your stupid body or your silly mind? It was to make her feel better. It was arranged. It was her idea, my friend, not mine. Possibly a silly idea, but she is desperate and unhappy and what else is there to do? But," she smiled thinly, "I will report a great success, a great rapture. I'm sure you won't be silly enough to contradict me. The lie will make her happy for a little while at least."

I had known it. I had suspected it. Or if I hadn't known it, was trying a similar grotesque test myself. Oh, the lunacy of the times!

"Now take your nasty bait and go and kill fish. The others will be here soon and I don't want them to see your miserable face."

I picked up the rod and a plastic bucket.

She called to me from the kitchen. "And put your worm back in your pants. It is singularly unattractive bait."

I said nothing and walked out the door with my cock sticking out of my fly. I found the dwarf standing on the landing. It gave him a laugh, at least.

8

I told her the truth about my encounter with the famous Jane Larange. I was a fool. I had made a worm to gnaw at her with fear and doubt. It burrowed into the space behind her eyes and secreted a filmy curtain of uncertainty and pain.

She became subject to moods which I found impossible to predict.

"Let me take your photograph," she said.

"Alright."

"Stand over there. No come down to the pier."

We went down to the pier.

"Alright."

"Now, take one of me."

"Where's the button?"

"On the top."

I found the button and took her photograph.

"Do you love me? Now?"

"Yes, damn you, of course I do."

She stared at me hard, tears in her eyes, then she wrenched the camera from my hand and hurled it into the water.

I watched it sink, thinking how beautifully clear the water was that day.

Carla ran up the steps to the house. I wasn't stupid enough to ask her what the matter was.

9

She had woken in one more mood, her eyes pale and staring and there was nothing I could do to reach her. There were only five days to go and these moods were thieving our precious time, arriving with greater frequency and lasting for longer periods.

I made the breakfast, frying bread in the bacon fat in a childish attempt to cheer her up. I detested these malignant withdrawals. They made her as blind and selfish as a baby.

She sat at the table, staring out the window at the water. I washed the dishes. Then I swept the floor. I was angry. I polished the floor and still she didn't move. I made the bed and cleaned down the walls in the bedroom. I took out all the books and put them in alaphabetical order according to author.

By lunchtime I was beside myself with rage.

She sat at the table.

I played a number of videotapes I knew she liked. She sat before the viewer like a blind deaf-mute. I took out a recipe book and began to prepare beef bourguignon with murder in my heart.

Then, some time about half-past two in the afternoon, she turned and said "Hello."

The cloud had passed. She stood and stretched and came and held me from behind as I cooked the beef.

"I love you," she said.

"I love you," I said.

She kissed me on the ear.

"What's the matter?" My rage had evaporated, but I still had to ask the stupid question.

"You know," she turned away from me and went to open the doors over the harbour. "Let's not talk about it."

"Well," I said, "maybe we should."

"Why?" she said. "I'm going to do it so there's nothing to be said."

I sat across from her at the table. "You're not going to go away," I said quietly, "and you are not going to take a Chance."

She looked up sharply, staring directly into my eyes, and I think then she finally knew that I was serious. We sat staring at each other, entering an unreal country as frightening as any I have ever travelled in.

Later she said quietly, "You have gone mad."

There was a time, before this one, when I never wept. But now as I nodded tears came, coursing down my cheeks. We held each other miserably, whispering things that mad people say to one another.

10

Orgasm curved above us and through us, carrying us into dark places where we spoke in tongues.

Carla, most beautiful of women, crying in my ear. "Tell me I'm beautiful."

Locked doors with broken hinges. Bank vaults blown asunder. Blasphemous papers floating on warm winds, lying in the summer streets, flapping like wounded seagulls.

11

In the morning the light caught her. She looked more beautiful than the Bonnards in Hale's *Critique of Bourgeois Art*, the orange sheet lying where she had kicked it, the fine hairs along her arm soft and golden in the early light.

Bonnard painted his wife for more than twenty years. Whilst her arse and tits sagged he painted her better and better. It made my eyes wet with sentimental tears to think of the old Mme. Bonnard posing for the ageing M. Bonnard, standing in the bathroom or sitting on the toilet seat of their tiny flat.

I was affected by visions of constancy. In the busy lanes behind the central market I watched an old couple helping each other along the broken-down pavement. He, short and stocky with a countryman's arms, now infirm and reduced to a walking stick. She, of similar height, overweight, carrying her shopping in an old-fashioned bag.

She walked beside him protectively, spying out broken cobblestones, steps, and the feet of beggars.

"You walk next to the wall," I heard her say, "I'll walk on the outside so no one kicks your stick again."

They swapped positions and set off once more, the old man jutting his chin, the old lady moving slowly on swollen legs, strangers to the mysteries of the Genetic Lottery and the glittering possibilities of a Chance.

When the sun, in time, caught Carla's beautiful face, she opened her eyes and smiled at me.

I felt so damned I wished to slap her face.

It was unbelievable that this should be taken from us. And even as I held her and kissed her sleep-soft lips, I was beginning, at last, to evolve a plan that would really keep her.

As I stroked her body, running one feathery finger down her shoulder, along her back, between her legs, across her thighs, I was designing the most intricate door, a door I could fit on the afternoon before her Chance-day, a door to keep her prisoner for a day at least. A door I could blame the landlord for, a door painted orange, a colour I could blame the painters for, a door to make her miss her appointment, a door that would snap shut with a normal click but would finally only yield to the strongest axe.

The idea, so clearly expressed, has all the tell-tale signs of total madness. Do not imagine I don't see that, or even that I didn't know it then. Emperors have built such monuments on grander scales and entered history with the grand expressions of their selfishness and arrogance.

So allow me to say this about my door: I am, even now, startled at the far-flung originality of the design and the obsessive craftsmanship I finally applied to its construction. Further: to this day I can think of no simpler method by which I might have kept her.

12

I approached the door with infinite cunning. I took a week off from work, telling Carla I had been temporarily suspended for insolence, something she found easy enough to believe.

On the first day I built a new door frame, thicker and heavier than the existing one and fixed it to the wall struts with fifty long brass screws. When I had finished I painted it with orange primer and rehung the old door.

"What's all this?" she asked.

"Those bloody painters are crazy," I said.

"But that's a new frame. Did the painters do that?"

"There was a carpenter, too," I said. "I wish you'd tell the landlord to stop it."

"I bought some beer," she said, "let's get drunk."

Neither of us wanted to talk about the door, but while we drank I watched it with satisfaction. The orange was a beautiful colour. It cheered me up no end.

13

The dwarf crept up on me and found me working on the plans for the door, sneaking up on his obscene little feet.

"Ah-huh."

I tried to hide it, this most complicated idea which was to lock you in, which on that very afternoon I would begin making in a makeshift workshop I had set up under the house. This gorgeous door of iron-hard old timber with its four concealed locks, their keyholes and knobs buried deep in the door itself.

"Ah," said the dwarf who had been a handsome fellow, resting his ugly little hand affectionately on my elbow. "Ah this is some door."

"It's for a friend," I said, silently cursing my carelessness. I should have worked under the house.

"More like an enemy," he observed. "With a door like that you could lock someone up in fine style, eh?"

I didn't answer. The dwarf was no fool but neither was he as crazy as I was. My secret was protected by my madness.

"Did it occur to you," the dwarf said, "that there might be a problem getting someone to walk through a doorway guarded by a door like this? A good trap should be enticing, or, at least, neutral, if you get my meaning."

"It is not for a jail," I said, "or a trap, either."

"You really should see someone," he said, sitting sadly on the low table.

"What do you mean, 'someone'?"

"Someone," he said, "who you could see. To talk to about your problems. A counsellor, a shrink, someone. . . ." He looked at me and smiled, lighting a stinking Fasta cigarette. "It's a beautiful door, just the same."

'Go and fuck yourself," I said, folding the plans. My fishing rod was in the corner.

"After the revolution," the dwarf said calmly, "there will be no locks. Children will grow up not understanding what a lock is. To see a lock it will be necessary to go to a museum."

"Would you mind passing me my fishing rod. It's behind you."

He obliged, making a small bow as he handed it over. "You should consider joining us," he said, "then you would not have this problem you have with Carla. There are bigger problems you could address your anger to. Your situation now is that you are wasting energy being angry at the wrong things."

"Go and fuck yourself," I smiled.

He shook his head. "Ah, so this is the level of debate we have come to. Go and fuck yourself, go and fuck yourself." He repeated my insult again and again, turning it over curiously in his mind.

I left him with it and went down to talk to the bream on the pier. When I saw him leave I went down below the house and spent the rest of the day cutting the timber for the door. Later I made dovetail joins in the old method before reinforcing them with steel plates for good measure.

14

The door lay beneath us, a monument to my duplicity and fear.

In a room above, clad by books, stroked slowly by Haydn, I presented this angry argument to her while she watched my face with wide wet eyes. "Don't imagine that you will forget all this.

85

Don't imagine it will all go away. For whatever comfort you find with your friends, whatever conscience you pacify, whatever guilt you assuage, you will always look back on this with regret, and know that it was unnecessary to destroy it. You will curse the schoolgirl morality that sent you to a Chance Centre and in your dreams you will find your way back to me and lie by my side and come fishing with me on the pier and everyone you meet you will compare and find lacking in some minor aspect."

I knew exactly how to frighten her. But the fear could not change her mind.

To my argument she replied angrily: "You understand nothing."

To which I replied: "You don't yet understand what you will understand in the end."

After she had finished crying we fucked slowly and I thought of Mme. Bonnard sitting on the edge of the bath, all aglow like a jewel.

15

She denied me a last night. She cheated me of it. She lied about the date of her Chance and left a day before she had said. I awoke to find only a note, carefully printed in a handwriting that seemed too young for the words it formed. Shivering, naked, I read it.

Dear Lumpy,
   You would have gone crazy. I know you. We couldn't part like that. I've seen the hate in your eyes but what I will remember is love in them after a beautiful fuck.

   I've got to be with Mum and Dad. When I see beggars in the street I think it's them. Can't you imagine how that feels? They have turned me into a Hup well and proper.

   You don't always give me credit for my ideas. You call me illogical, idealist, fool. I think you think they all mean the same thing. They don't. I have no illusions (and I don't just mean the business about being sick that you mentioned). Now when I walk down the street people smile at me easily. If I want help it comes easily. It is possible for me to do things like borrow money from strangers. I feel loved and protected. This is the privilege of my body which I must renounce. There is no choice. But it would be a mistake for you to imagine that I haven't thought properly about what I am doing. I am terrified and cannot change my mind.

There is no one I have known who I have ever loved a thousandth as much as you. You would make a perfect Hup. You do not judge, you are objective, compassionate. For a while I thought we could convert you, but c'est la vie. You are a tender lover and I am crying now, thinking how I will miss you. I am not brave enough to risk seeing you in whatever body the comrades can extract from the Fastas. I know your feelings on these things. It would be too much to risk. I couldn't bear the rejection.

I love you, I understand you.

Carla.

I crumpled it up. I smoothed it out. I kept saying "Fuck" repeating the word meaninglessly, stupidly, with anger one moment, pain the next. I dressed and ran out to the street. The bus was just pulling away. I ran through the early morning streets to the Chance Centre, hoping she hadn't gone to another district to confuse me. The cold autumn air rasped my lungs, and my heart pounded wildly. I grinned to myself thinking it would be funny for me to die of a heart attack. Now I can't think why it seemed funny.

16

Even though it was early the Chance Centre was busy. The main concourse was crowded with people waiting for relatives, staring at the video display terminals for news of their friends' emergence. The smell of trauma was in the air, reminiscent of stale orange peel and piss. Poor people in carpet slippers with their trousers too short sat hopefully in front of murals depicting Leonardo's classic proportions. Fasta technicians in grubby white coats wheeled patients in and out of the concourse in a sequence as aimless and purposeless as the shuffling of a deck of cards. I could find Carla's name on none of the terminals.

I waited the morning. Nothing happened. The cards were shuffled. The coffee machine broke down. In the afternoon I went out and bought a six-pack of beer and a bottle of Milocaine capsules.

17

In the dark, in the night, something woke me. My tongue furry, my eyes like gravel, my head still dulled from the dope and drink, half-conscious I half saw the woman sitting in the chair by the bed.

A fat woman, weeping.

I watched her like television. A blue glow from the neon lights in the street showed the coarse, folded surface of her face, her poor lank greying hair, deep creases in her arms and fingers like the folds in babies' skin, and the great drapery of chin and neck was reminiscent of drought-resistant cattle from India.

It was not a fair time, not a fair test. I am better than that. It was the wrong time. Undrugged, ungrogged, I would have done better. It is unreasonable that such a test should come in such a way. But in the deep grey selfish folds of my mean little brain I decided that I had not woken up, that I would wake up. I groaned, feigning sleep and turned over.

Carla stayed by my bed till morning, weeping softly while I lay with my eyes closed, sometimes sleeping, sometimes listening.

In the full light of morning she was gone and had, with bitter reproach, left behind merely one thing: a pair of her large grey knickers, wet with the juices of her unacceptable desire. I placed them in the rubbish bin and went out to buy some more beer.

18

I was sitting by the number five pier finishing off the last of the beer. I didn't feel bad. I'd felt a damn sight worse. The sun was out and the light dancing on the water produced a light dizzy feeling in my beer-sodden head. Two bream lay in the bucket, enough for my dinner, and I was sitting there pondering the question of Carla's flat: whether I should get out or whether I was meant to get out or whether I could afford to stay on. They were not difficult questions but I was managing to turn them into major events. Any moment I'd be off to snort a couple more caps of Milocaine and lie down in the sun.

I was not handling this well.

"Two fish, eh?"

I looked up. It was the fucking dwarf. There was nothing to say to him.

He sat down beside me, his grotesque little legs hanging over the side of the pier. His silence suggested a sympathy I did not wish to accept from him.

"What do you want, ugly?"

"It's nice to hear that you've finally relaxed, mm? Good to see that you're not pretending any more." He smiled. He seemed not in the least malicious. "I have brought the gift."

"A silly custom. I'm surprised you follow it." It was customary for people who took the Chance to give their friends pieces of clothing from their old bodies, clothing that they expected wouldn't fit the new. It had established itself as a pressure-cooked folk custom, like brides throwing corsages and children putting first teeth under their pillows.

The dwarf held out a small brown-paper parcel.

I unwrapped the parcel while he watched. It contained a pair of small white lady's knickers. They felt as cold and vibrant as echoes across vast canyons: quavering questions, cries, and thin, misunderstandings.

I shook the dwarf by his tiny hand.

The fish jumped forlornly in the bucket.

18

So long ago. So much past. Furies, rages, beer and sleeping pills. They say that the dwarf was horribly tortured during the revolution, that his hands were literally sawn from his arms by the Fastas. The hunchback lady now adorns the 50 IG postage stamps, in celebration of her now famous role at the crucial battle of Haytown.

And Carla, I don't know. They say there was a fat lady who was one of the fiercest fighters, who attacked and killed without mercy, who slaughtered with rage that was exceptional even in such a bloody time.

But I, I'm a crazy old man, alone with his books and his beer and his dog. I have been a clerk and a pedlar and a seller of cars. I have been ignorant, and a scholar of note. Pock-marked and ugly I have wandered the streets and slept in the parks. I have been bankrupt and handsome and a splendid con-man. I have been a river of poisonous silver mercury, without form or substance, yet I carry with me this one pain, this one yearning, that I love you, my lady, with all my heart. And on evenings when the water is calm and the birds dive amongst the whitebait, my eyes swell with tears as I think of you sitting on a chair beside me, weeping in a darkened room.

The Puzzling Nature of Blue

Part 1

Vincent is crying again. Bloody Vincent. Here I am, a woman of thirty-five, and I still can't handle a fool like Vincent. He's like a yellow dog, one of those curs who hangs around your back door for scraps and you feed him once, you show him a little affection, and he stays there. He's yours. You're his. Bloody Vincent, crying by the fire, and spilling his drink again.

It began as stupidly as you'd expect a thing like that to begin. There was no way in which it could have begun intelligently. Vincent put an ad in the *Review*: Home and companionship wanted for ex-drunken Irish poet shortly to be released from Long Bay. Apply V. Day Box 37320.

I did it. I answered it. And now Vincent is crying by the fire and spilling his drink and all I can say is, "Get the Wettex."

He nods his head determinedly through his tears, struggles to get up, and falls over. He knocks his head on the table. I find it impossible to believe that he hasn't choreographed the whole sequence but I'm the one who gets up and fetches the Wettex. I use it to wipe up the blood on his head. God save me.

Yesterday I kicked him out. So he began to tear down the brick wall he'd started to build for me. Then he gave up and started crying. The crying nauseated me. But I couldn't kick him out. It was the fifth time I couldn't kick him out.

I'm beginning to wonder if I'm not emotionally dependent on the drama he provides me. What other reason is there for keeping him here? Perhaps it's as simple as pity. I know how bad he is. Anyone who knew him well wouldn't let him in the door. I have fantasies about Vincent sleeping with the winos in the park. I refuse to have that on my head.

"How many people answered your ad?" I asked.

"Only you."

Thus he makes even his successes sound pitiful.

Tonight I have made a resolution, to exploit Vincent to the same extent that he has exploited me. He has a story or two to tell. He is not a poet. He was never in Long Bay. But he has a story or two. One of those interests me. I intend to wring this story from Vincent as I wring this Wettex, marked with his poor weak blood, amongst the dirty dishes in the kitchen sink.

Before I go any further though, in my own defence, I intend to make a list of Vincent's crimes against me, for my revenge will not be inconsiderable and I have the resources to inflict serious injuries upon him.

Vincent's first crime was to lie to me about having been in Long Bay, to ask for sympathy on false grounds, to say he was a poet when he wasn't, to say he was a reformed alcoholic when he was a soak.

Vincent's second crime was to inflict his love on me when I had no wish for it. He used his dole money to send me flowers and stole my own money to buy himself drink. He stole my books and (I suppose) sold them. He gave my records to a man in the pub, so he says, and if that's what he says then the real thing is worse.

Vincent's third crime was to tell Paul that I loved him (Vincent) and that I was trying to mother him, and because I was mothering him he couldn't write any more.

Vincent's fourth crime was to perform small acts that would make me indebted to him in some way. Each time he demanded some extraordinary payment for his troubles. The wall he is propped against now is an example. He built this wall because he thought I couldn't. I was pleased. It seemed a selfless act and perhaps I saw it as some sort of repayment for my care of him. But building the wall somehow, in Vincent's mind, was related to him sleeping with me. When I said "no" he began to tear down the wall and call me a cock-teaser. The connection between the wall and my bed may seem extreme but it was perfectly logical to Vincent who has always known that there is a price for everything.

Vincent's fifth crime was his remorse for all his other crimes.

His remorse was more cloying, more clinging, more suffocating, more pitiful than any of his other actions and it was, he knew, the final imprisoning act. He knows that no matter how hardened I might become to everything else the display of remorse always works. He knows that I suspect it is false remorse, but he also knows that I am not really sure and that I'll always give him the benefit of the doubt.

Vincent is crying again. I'd chuck him out but he's got nowhere else to go and I've got nothing else to trouble me.

I can't guarantee the minor details of what follows. I've put it together from what Vincent has told me and checked it against what he's told others. Often he's contradicted himself. Often he's got the dates wrong. Sometimes he tells me that it was he who suggested Upward Island, sometimes he tells me that the chairman mumbled something about it and no one else heard it.

So what happens here, in this reconstruction, is based on what I know of the terrible Vincent, not what I know of the first board meeting he ever went to, a brand new director who was, even then, involved with the anti-war movement.

The first board meeting Vincent ever went to took place when the Upward Island Republic was still plain Upward Island, a little dot on the map to the north of Australia. I guess Vincent was much the same as he is now, not as pitiful, not as far gone, less of a professional Irishman, but still as burdened with the guilt that he carries around so proudly to this day. It occurs to me that he was, even then, looking for things to be guilty about.

Allow for my cynicism about him. Vincent was never, no matter what I say, a fool. I have heard him spoken of as a first-rate economist. He had worked in senior positions for two banks and as a policy adviser to the Labour Party. In addition, if he's to be believed, he was a full board member of Farrow (Australasia) at thirty-five. It is difficult to imagine an American company giving a position to someone like Vincent, no matter how clever. But Farrow were English and it is remotely possible that they didn't know about his association with the anti-war movement, his tendency to drink too much, and his unstable home life.

In those days he had no beard. He wore tailored suits from Eugenio Medecini and ate each day at a special table at the

Florentino. He may have seemed a little too smooth, a trifle insincere, but that is probably to underestimate his not inconsiderable talent for charm.

Which brings us back at last to the time of the first board meeting.

Vincent was nervous. He had been flattered and thrilled to be appointed to the board. He was also in the habit of saying that he had compromised his principles by accepting it. In the month that elapsed between his appointment and the first meeting his alternate waves of elation and guilt gave way to more general anxiety.

He was worried, as usual, that he wasn't good enough, that he would make a fool of himself by saying the wrong thing, that he wouldn't say anything, that he would be expected to perform little rituals the nature of which he would be unfamiliar with.

The night before he went out on a terrible drunk with his ex-wife and her new lover, during which he became first grandiose and then pathetic. They took him home and put him to bed. The next morning he woke with the painful clarity he experienced in those days from a hangover, a clarity he claimed helped him write better.

He shaved without cutting himself and dressed in the fawn gaberdine suit which he has often described to me in loving detail. I know little about the finer details of the construction of men's suits, so I can't replay the suit to you stitch for stitch the way Vincent, slumped on the floor in his stained old yellow T-shirt and filthy jeans, has done for me. I sometimes think that the loss of that suit has been one of the great tragedies of Vincent's life, greater than the loss of his wife Jenny to Frank, greater than the loss of his fictitious manuscripts which he claims he left on a Pioneer bus between Coffs Harbour and Lismore.

But on the day of his first board meeting the suit was still his and he dressed meticulously, tying a big knot in the Pierre Cardin tie that Jenny and Frank had given him to celebrate his appointment. His head was calm and clear and he ignored the Enthal asthma inhaler which lay on his dresser and caught a cab to the office.

Whenever Vincent talks about the meeting his attitude to the events is ambivalent and he alternates between pride and self-hatred as he relates it. He has pride in his mental techniques and hatred for the results of those techniques.

"As a businessman," he is fond of saying, "I was a poet, but as a poet, I was a fucking whore." He explains the creative process to me in insulting detail, with the puzzled pride of someone explaining colour to the blind. He is eager that business be seen as a creative act. He quotes Koestler (who I know he has never read) on the creative process and talks about the joining of unlikely parts together to create a previously unknown whole.

There were a number of minor matters on the early part of the agenda, the last of which was a letter from the manager of the works at Upward Island. Upward was a vestige of an earlier empire when the company had been heavily involved in sugar, pearling, and other colonial enterprises. Now it was more an embarrassment than a source of profit and no one knew what to do with it. No one in the company was directly responsible for affairs there which is why such a trivial matter was now being referred to the full board for a decision.

The letter from the manager complained about pilferage from the company stores. He apologized profusely for the trouble he was causing but stressed at the same time the importance of his complaint. The natives had less and less respect for the company and were now stealing not only rum (which was traditional and accepted) but many other things for which they could have no conceivable use. For instance a whole case of 25 amp fuses had disappeared and their absence had put the company Land-Rover out of action. The manager was now forced to travel around the island by mule, a sight which caused him much embarrassment and the natives much amusement.

Vincent, cool and professional in his new suit, searched his mind for some dramatically simple answer to this problem, but he came up with nothing. When the chairman asked him his opinion, he felt embarrassed to say that he could think of nothing.

As usual with matters concerning Upward Island, the matter was delegated to the chairman's secretary who would, it was expected, send the manager a beautifully typed and completely useless letter.

With the matter of Upward Island thus disposed of, the next item on the agenda was considered. This was a problem which caused the board some serious anxiety and was to do with two million dollars worth of Eupholon which was at this moment on the seas and heading for Australia.

You may or may not be aware of the nature of Eupholon. There was some coverage in the international press when the American Food and Drug Administration committee ordered its withdrawal from the U.S. market and most western governments followed suit. During the late sixties Eupholon had been prescribed as a central nervous system stimulant not unrelated to amphetamines. However prolonged use of the drug produced a number of nasty side effects, the most dramatic of these being a violent blue colour in the extremities of the body. Normally the fingers and hands were first affected, but cases of feet, noses and ears were also mentioned in the reports.

Farrow International was thus left with an inventory of millions of dollars worth of Eupholon which it had little hope of selling but which it also refused to destroy. The Birmingham head office lived in the fond hope that the Food and Drug Administration's earlier decision would be reversed. However the drug was still legally available in Australia, and the U.K. office, in an attempt to minimize in losses, had planned a big push on the Australian market. The two million dollar shipment at present on the water was to be sold in the first six months.

Unfortunately the Australian government had banned the drug soon after the ship entered the Pacific. And now the Australian board was meeting to decide what to do with such a large quantity of such an undesirable drug.

The international directive was to warehouse it and wait. But warehouse space in Melbourne and Sydney was at a premium and the cost of hiring space for what might be an indefinite period gave the board members worried faces and expensive frowns.

It was then that Vincent asked his question about Upward Island which, at first, seemed so irrelevant that nobody bothered to answer him. His question had been about harbour facilities.

The chairman reminded him that the Upward Island matter had been settled but Vincent insisted on an answer and was told that Upward Island had an excellent harbour.

He then asked about the company store.

He was told that the company store was very large indeed.

Could it accommodate the Eupholon?

Yes, it could.

Could the ship be diverted to Upward?

Yes, it could.

Vincent must have smirked. He would have felt it childish to smile, and his repressed smiles look like nasty little smirks. So I can see the board members looking with wonder at his face, not knowing whether to be pleased with his suggestion or irritated by the smirk.

Vincent had solved the problem but he was not content to leave it at that and, in a demonstration of his creative genius, went on to spell out the ramifications of this plan.

The problem of pilferage on Upward Island would be simply cured. When the Eupholon arrived it would certainly be subject to pilferage. This in itself didn't matter and would hardly occasion huge losses, but perhaps this pilfering could be used to stop other pilfering.

Assuming the islanders maintained their habits (the manager, in a crude attempt at humour, had euphemistically detailed the effects on several men who had stolen a carton of laxatives) then whoever stole the Eupholon would quickly become visible. Their hands would turn blue. They would not only become visible to the authorities but would provide a living demonstration of the powers of the company to mark those who transgressed its laws.

Thus, Vincent explained, the two problems could be solved at once. Pilferage on Upward Island would be prevented effectively and the Eupholon could be warehoused at no extra cost to the company.

It seems likely that no one gave a damn about the pilferage problem, but Vincent was so obviously thrilled with the neatness of his solution and they were so grateful for a place to put the Eupholon that they were in no mood to nit-pick or to criticize the more far-fetched aspects of the scheme.

As soon as his plan was formally adopted and a cable sent to Birmingham with a request to re-route the ship, Vincent was immediately stricken with terrible remorse. He had fallen, once more, victim to his own terrible brilliance. He had helped a colonial power (Farrow) wreak havoc and injury on an innocent people (the Upward Islanders) and he had been proud to do it.

The thought of those islanders walking around with blue hands suddenly seemed obscene and terrible to him and he immediately sent a memo to the managing director wherein he requested that an armed guard be placed on the warehouse at all times and that the man be given instructions to shoot anyone attempting to enter the warehouse without proper reason. He was confident that one wounding (unfortunate though that might be) would act as an effective deterrent and prevent the realization of the nightmare he had created. He investigated the award rates for armed guards and included in his memo a breakdown of all costs involved in the scheme. The amounts were so minor that the matter was approved without comment, although it seems likely that Vincent was pushing the Upward Island idea to the point where it would become a private joke amongst his fellow directors.

Satisfied with all this Vincent went off to a meeting of the Vietnam Moratorium Committee where, dressed in faded jeans and a blue workshirt, he was among those who supported a call for physical confrontation with the police. Excepting the few who suspected he was an agent provocateur, those who saw him speak were impressed by the emotion of his appeal and the fact that there were tears in his eyes when he spoke about the Vietnamese people.

It would be wrong to think that the tears were false or his appeal cynical. Vincent was continually in a state of conflict between his heartfelt principles and his need to be well thought of by people.

I don't think that there's any need to say any more about Vincent's life at this time. The shipment duly arrived at Upward Island and was stored as expected. Considerable quantities of Eupholon were stolen. Several islanders were shot dead by over-zealous guards, many were wounded.

It is thought that the Gilbert and Sullivan revolution which took place on Upward Island last week may well have been directly attributable to these shootings. Vincent himself chooses to believe this, which is no reason for believing that it isn't true. Certainly it was a painless revolution and the small island, against the advice but not the wishes of the Australian government, was granted its independence. The company was expelled and its stocks of Eupholon confiscated. This caused Farrow International no pains at all as by this time it had become obvious, even to Birmingham, that Eupholon would never be acceptable to the market again.

Reports of the revolution have noted the blue hands of certain members of the revolution, but these have been generally described in the press as "war-paint".

It is on account of those blue hands that Vincent is sitting in my room and weeping.

In the year that has elapsed since the first board meeting he has slowly and gracefully slid downhill. He became more and more outspoken in his anti-war activities until such time as these activities became an embarrassment to the company and he was fired on the direct instruction of Birmingham. It is perhaps unfortunate that at the same time the members of the Moratorium Committee discovered that he was actually a director of Farrow (whose French subsidiary was actively involved in the production of chemical warfare agents) and expelled him for his moral duplicity.

With these two emotional props removed Vincent went to pieces. He departed for Queensland to write but only got as far as Lismore where he was looked after briefly by communards.

His memory of events after this time is either unclear or so embarrassing to him that he is not prepared to reveal any significant details. He still insists that it all came to a climax two months ago with him being interned in Long Bay for assaulting a policeman at a demonstration, but I know this is untrue. It is possible he would have liked the idea of going to Long Bay, but he never has.

Now I can let you into a secret.

This is something I've been hoping might happen as I've worked. Had it not happened, this little account of Vincent's involvement with Upward Island would still have been of some real interest. However, recent events mean that I may be able to pursue the matter in a more purposeful way.

Vincent assaulted me last night. He came home with some people I'd never seen before, demanded I feed them, abused me when I refused, and punched me in the mouth when they left.

I'm afraid that I am now angry with him, I can no longer be

dispassionate. The tiny part of me that observed Vincent with god-like pity has gone. I talked of revenge before. I was speaking of some minor bitching revenge of exploiting his story for my own gain. Now, however, I have a broken tooth which will have to be capped. It'll cost me two hundred dollars. My warfare with Vincent has come into the open.

I have told him to go and I will not change my mind. He knows it. At this moment his bags are packed but he is staying to finish dismantling the brick wall, a job he does with sullen thoroughness. He watches me typing over the top of it, a self-satisfied smirk on his face. I'd love to know what he thought he was doing with that brick wall. I'm sure it represents all kinds of incredible things for him. There is mortar dust over the dishes in the kitchen and all the furniture. There is mortar dust over the typewriter and between my teeth.

Well, Vincent my friend, the paper I work for is committed to sending me to Upward Island to look at this quaint little revolution. And now I've got a little background information from you, I'll use it and broaden it in the best way I can. I shall publicize you, Vincent, both here and on Upward Island. I'm sure the leaders of Upward Island will be most interested to know who is responsible for their blue hands. I'm not sure if you're legally responsible but I'm sure you should be.

Part 2

I have led you on with promises of a spectacular revenge, and now I will tell you that there shall be no revenge. Instead, I hope, a more substantial meal awaits you.

In four days on Upward Island I have seen three months' planning come undone. Am I so shallow, so easily swayed? Am I like an adolescent girl, jumping from love to hatred with every change in the weather?

Whatever my mental balance, there is more than a little explaining to do. Vincent is sitting on my bed in the Rainbow Motel, Upward Island. The fan turns overhead. The cockroaches stroll casually across the concrete floor. In the corner, above the basin, a little lizard lies, occasionally making small bird noises.

Vincent informs me that he is a chee-chuk.

He leans back against the pillow and I observe for the twentieth time what I never saw until this week: what lovely legs he has: long, slim straight legs as deeply tanned as rich students on long holidays. He looks so clean, so healthy. His beard is gone and there is no longer anything to veil his fine sensitive chiselled features with those beautiful sad grey eyes. Vincent, did I tell you that even when I was most angry with you I loved your eyes? They are less of an enigma to me now.

We have not arrived easily at this still, calm moment in this little room. We have travelled via suspicion and rage. I have watched him, on other days, as he earnestly helped me prepare my article, providing me with facts I hadn't known about his past, and easing my way into knowledge of his present. He has acted as my guide and denied me nothing and I watched carefully for his sleight of hand as he prepared the scaffolding for his own execution.

But there have been no tricks. Neither has there been remorse, tears, demands, or violence.

Instead I have come to envy him his calm, his contentment, his ability to sit still and keep his silence.

Vincent left for Upward Island on the day I threw him out. He had been planning it from the time he met me. He paid for the fare with money from my stolen books and records and a number of even less savoury transactions. I can imagine him arriving: bedraggled, dirty, full of guilt and speed in equal proportions, going from one bar to the next in search of someone who would forgive him the sin he hadn't the courage to confess. He had no money, no plan, and existed in drunken agony at the bottom of the big black pit he had built for himself. He had come, classically, with remorse, but the remorse would not go away and with each day he fell further and further into the grips of despair. He couldn't leave. It was impossible to stay.

It was finally Solly Ling, the new president himself, who picked him up off the floor and took him home. Taking him for a derelict (which he was) Solly set about drying him out. He found him clothes and gave him food and then, sternly, put him to work.

Vincent had never done sustained physical labour in his life. But now he was forced to work on the building of the Upward

Island school. There was no alternative. He dug stump holes until his hands were raw and bleeding. He carried bricks until his arms only existed as a nagging pain in his brain. He poured concrete.

He spoke little and never complained. There was a logic in it. It was a penance. He accepted it.

Solly had cleared out an old shed in his backyard and there Vincent, wide-eyed and sleepless, listened with terror to toads and rats and flying foxes and other nocturnal mysteries slither and flap and eat and dig around the hut.

Vincent and Solly ate together, mostly in silence, for Vincent was terrified of revealing anything of his past. But Solly was a patient man and a curious one. He sensed Vincent's education and with one question one day and another the next he finally learned that Vincent was a lawyer and an economist, that he had worked for big companies including several banks. At that time the island council was making heavy weather of the constitution and one night Solly broached the subject with Vincent and he watched with pleasure as Vincent took the thing apart and put it together in a neat, simple and logical way. The next day Vincent met the council. He was patient and self-effacing. Solly watched him and saw a sensitive diplomat, a man who listened to every speaker and was able to see the value of a sensible objection, but who could also politely point out the disadvantages of a less sensible one.

It was a touchy business. The council could have rejected him, found him patronizing, or too clever by half. But none of these things happened. Vincent's guilt had made his nerve ends as raw as his blistered hands and he felt their feelings with a peculiar intensity. He acted as a servant, never once imposing his own will.

His service to the council, however, was but a drop of water on the fires of his guilt. He sat in the old Waterside Workers Union shed where the council meetings were held and all he could see were the blue hands of the councillors. Surrounded by the evidence of his crime there was no room for escape.

He drafted three new prawning contracts and volunteered for the unpleasant job of cleaning the mortar off the old bricks for the school. He painted Solly's house for him and went on to start the vegetable garden.

These acts were in no way intended to curry favour or gain friendship (in fact they were some sort of substitute for wrath) but they succeeded in spite of that. The islanders took to him: not only was he educated but he was also prepared to work at the nastiest jobs side by side with them, he could tell funny stories, he didn't flirt with their wives, and he'd negotiated the best damn prawn contracts they'd ever had.

It is doubtful if Vincent noticed this. He was not accustomed to being liked and would have never expected it on Upward Island.

Given his skills, it's natural enough that he should have been co-opted as an assistant to the council. But that he should be elected formally to the council after only two months in an indication of the popularity he had begun to enjoy. Again, it is doubtful if he saw it.

On the night after his election to the council he sat on the verandah with Solly and looked out at the approaching night, a night that was still foreign to him and full of things he neither liked nor understood.

Solly was a big man. The stomach that bulged beneath his white singlet betrayed his love of beer, just as the muscular forearms attested to his years as a waterside worker. The great muscled calves that protruded from his rolled-up trousers were the legs of a young man, but the creased black face and the curly greying hair betrayed his age. It was a face that could show, almost simultaneously, the dignity of a judge and the bright-eyed recklessness of a born larrikin.

He sat on the verandah of his high-stilted house, one big blue hand around a beer bottle, the other around a glass which he filled and passed to Vincent. The hand which took the glass was now calloused and tough. The arm, never thick, was now wiry and hard, tatooed with knicks and scratches and dusty with mortar. A flea made its way through the hairs and dust on the arm. Vincent saw it and knocked it off. It wasn't worth killing them. There were too many.

As the darkness finally shrouded the garden a great clamour began in the hen house.

"Bloody python," said Solly.

"I'll go." Vincent stood up. He didn't want to go. He hadn't gone yet, but it was about time he went.

"I'll go." Solly picked up a shotgun and walked off into the dark. Vincent sipped his beer and knew that next time he'd have to go.

There was a shot and Solly came back holding the remains of a python in one hand and a dead chicken in the other.

"Too late," he grinned, "snake got him first."

He sat down, leaving the dead bird on the floor, and the snake draped across the railing.

"Now you're on the council," he said, "we're going to have to do something to get your hands in shape."

"Ah, they're all right. The blisters have all gone." Vincent wondered what blisters had to do with the council.

"I wasn't talking about blisters, Mr. Economics. I was discussing the matter of your hands." Solly chuckled. His white teeth flashed in the light from the kitchen window. "You're going to have to take some medicine."

Vincent was used to being teased. He had faced poisonous grasshoppers, threatened cyclones and dozens of other tricks they liked to play on him. He didn't know what this was about, but he'd find out soon enough.

"What medicine is that, Sol?"

"Why," laughed Solly, "little pills, of course. You need a few little pills now you're on the council. We can't have you sitting on the council with the wrong-coloured hands."

Vincent couldn't believe what he was hearing. They'd never discussed the blue hands. His mind had been full of it. Not a day had gone by when the blue hands hadn't caused him pain. But he had avoided mentioning them for fear of touching so nasty a wound.

"Eupholon?" He said it. The word.

"For a smart boy you're very slow. Sure, that's what they call it."

Vincent's scalp prickled. He had said the name. How did he know the name? They knew about him. It was a trap. Now it would be the time for justice to be done. They would force him to take the poison he'd given them.

There was a silence.

"Solly, you know where I worked before?"

"Sure, you was the great Economics man."

"I mean what company?"

"Sure, you worked for Mr. Farrow." Solly's voice was calm, but Vincent's ears were ringing in the silence between the words.

"How you know that, Solly?"

"Oh, you got a lady friend who reckons you're a bad fella. She wrote us a letter. Three pages. Boy, what you do to her, eh?" He laughed again. "She's a very angry lady, that one."

"Anita."

"I forget her name," he waved an arm, dismissing it. "Some name like that."

In the corner of his eye, Vincent saw the headless python twitch.

"That why you want me to take the pills?"

"Christ no." Solly roared with laughter, a great whooping laugh that slid from a wheezing treble to deepest bass. "Christ no, you crazy bastard." He stood up and came and sat by Vincent on the step, hugging him. "You crazy Economics bastard, no." He wiped his eyes with a large blue hand. "Oh shit. You are what they call a one-off model. You know what that means?"

"What?" Vincent was numb, almost beyond speech.

"It means you are fucking unique. I love you."

Vincent was very confused. He slapped at a few mosquitoes and tried to puzzle it out. Every shred of fact that his life was based on seemed as insubstantial as fairy floss. "You don't care I sent the pills here?"

"Care!" the laughter came again. "To put it properly to you, we are fucking delighted you sent the pills here. Everything is fine. Why should we be mad with you?"

"The blue hands . . ."

"You are not only crazy," said Solly affectionately. "You are also nine-tenths blind. Don't you notice anything about the blue hands?"

"What do you mean?"

"I mean you're bloody blind. All the best men got blue hands. All the bravest men. We're bloody proud of these hands. You got blue hands on Upward, Vincent, you got respect. How come you can live here so long and not notice that? We had to beat that damn guard to get these hands, Vincent. When the time came to kick out Farrow, everyone knows who's got the guts to do it, because we're the only ones that's got the hands."

"So I've got to have blue hands, to be on the council?"

"You got it. You got perfect understanding."

"OK," Vincent grinned. He felt as light as air. He poured himself another beer. He wanted to get drunk and sing songs. He didn't dwell on the idea of the blue hands. That was nothing. All he said was, "Where do I get the pills?"

Solly scratched his head. "Well, I suppose there must be some up at the warehouse. You better go up and take a look."

Vincent started laughing then, laughing with pure joy and relief. The more he thought about it, the funnier it was and the more he laughed. And Solly sitting beside him, laughed too.

I imagine the pair of them hooting and cackling into the dark tropical night, a dead chicken at their feet, a headless python twitching on the railing. Not surprisingly, they were laughing about different things.

Late the next morning Vincent set off to walk to the warehouse. He felt marvellous. In the kitchen he cut himself some sandwiches and on the dusty road he found a long stick. He walked the three mile track with a light heart, delighting in the long seas of golden grass, finding beauty in the muddy mangrove shoreline and its heat-hazed horizon.

Vincent in white shorts with his cut lunch and walking stick like a tourist off to visit Greek ruins.

The warehouse shone silver in the harsh midday sun. There was something written on the side. As he came up the last steep slope he finally made it out: someone had painted a blue hand on the longest side of the building and added, for good measure: WARNING—DEATH. He wondered vaguely if this had been the manager's work. How gloriously ineffective it had been. What total misunderstanding had been displayed.

He was still a hundred yards from the warehouse when he saw a man, dressed in white shorts like himself, standing at the front of the building.

The man called.

Vincent waved casually and continued on, wondering who it

was. The man was white. He had seen no white people until now.

As he walked up the hill, being careful not to slip on the shale which made up the embankment, the man disappeared for a second and then came back with what looked like a rifle. Vincent's first thought was: a snake, he's seen a snake. He grasped his stick firmly and walked ahead, his eyes on the ground in front of him.

So he didn't see the man lift the rifle to his shoulder and fire.

The bullet hit the ground a yard ahead of him and ricocheted dangerously off the rocks.

Vincent stopped and yelled. The man was a lunatic. The bloody thing had nearly got him. Even as he shouted he saw him raise the rifle again.

This time he felt the wind of the bullet next to his cheek.

He didn't stay to argue any longer, he turned to run, fell, dropped the sandwiches and stick and slithered belly down over shale for a good twenty feet. When he stood up it was to run.

From the next hill he saw the man with the gun walk down the hill, pick up the sandwiches and slowly saunter back to the warehouse.

Imagine Vincent, cut, bruised, covered in sweat, his eyes wide with outrage and anger as he strode into the Royal Hotel and found Solly at the bar.

"Solly, there's some crazy bastard at the warehouse. He shot at me. With a fucking rifle."

"No," said Solly, his eyes wide.

"Yes," said Vincent. "The bugger could have killed me."

They bought drinks for Vincent that night and he finally learned that the guards he had once employed for Farrow were now employed by the council to continue their valuable work. Those with blue hands did not want them devalued.

And Vincent, nursing his bruises at the bar, tried to smile at the joke. It was not going to be as easy to get his blue hands as he'd thought.

Faced with the terrifying prospect of death or wounding, he began to consider the possibility of blue hands more carefully.

Whilst they would give him some prestige on Upward Island, they would make him grotesque anywhere else, of interest only to doctors and laughing schoolchildren on buses. He saw himself in big cities on summer days, wearing white gloves like Mickey Mouse. He saw the embarrassed eyes of people he knew and, he says, my own triumphant face as I revelled in the irony of it: Dr Strangelove with radiation poisoning.

If there had been anywhere left to run to, he would have gone. If there was a job he could have taken, he would have taken it. Even without this, he would have gone, if he'd had the money.

But he had no money. No chance of a job. And he was forced to consider what he would do.

And as he thought about it, lying on his bed, drinking with Solly, nailing down the roof of the schoolhouse, he came to realize that not only couldn't he leave, he didn't want to. He came to see that he was liked, respected, even loved. For the first time in his life he considered the possibility of happiness. It was a strange thing for him to look at, and he examined it with wonder.

What was so wrong with Upward Island?

He couldn't think of anything.

Did he miss the city? Not particularly. Did he miss friends? He didn't have any. Did he miss success? He had failed. Strangely, he had become somebody: he was Vince, he worked down at the school, he cleaned bricks, he did the prawn contracts.

On the morning of the second day after the shooting he came to the realization that he had no option but to stay. And if he was to stay he had no option but to get his hands the right colour. He looked the prospect of the warehouse in the eye and was filled with terror at what he saw.

Vincent was frightened of snakes, lizards, bats, spiders, scorpions, large ants, and noises in the night he didn't understand. He used what daylight he could and crept to the point in the track where the warehouse was just visible, then he sat on a rock and waited for darkness.

His face and hands were blackened. His shirt sleeves were long. In his pocket he carried the torch Solly had given him. As the sun set a crow flew across the sky, uttering a cry so forlorn that it struck a chill in Vincent's heart.

The sky turned from melodramatic red, to grey, and slowly to darkness. He edged painfully up the path convinced he would put his hand on a snake. A rustle in the grass kept him immobile for two minutes. He stared into the darkness with his hair bristling. A toad jumped across his boot and he slipped backwards in fright. He pressed on, crawling. His hand grasped a nettle. A sharp rock pierced his trousers and tore his skin. Tiny pieces of gravel inflicted a hundred minor tortures on his naked hands. A flying fox, its wings as loud as death itself, flew over him on its way to a wild guava bush.

Yet there were few noises loud enough to distract him from his beating heart. It felt as if his head was full of beating blood.

Slowly, very slowly, he edged his way to the warehouse. Once it had been nothing more than a word in a memo, but now it gleamed horribly under a bright moon, the colourless words on its side clearly visible and exactly calculated in their effect.

The guards were well paid and took three shifts. They were established in very good houses, were given three months' holiday a year and were encouraged to bring their families to Upward. They were stable, serious men, and if they mixed little in the society, they were certainly vital to it.

Tonight it was Van Dogen. They had teased Vincent about this, saying Van Dogen was the best shot of them all.

He could hear Van Dogen above him, walking up and down on the gravel. Once his face flared white from the darkness as he lit a cigarette. Vincent watched the tiny red speck of cigarette as it swung around the building like a deadly firefly.

Now, he made his way slowly to where there was no red dot, to the back of the warehouse where the water tank stood. For here, he knew, was the way to the roof. On to the wooden stand, then to the tank, a slow dangerous arm-lift to the roof. Now he moved on borrowed sandshoes across the vast expanse of metal roof, a loud footstep disguised by the noises caused by the contraction of the metal in the cool night air.

The third skylight from the end awaited him as promised. He climbed through slowly and his dangling feet found the rafter. Slowly, quietly, he closed the skylight and giddily, fearfully, lowered himself from the rafter.

He let go, hoping the superphosphate sacks were still below.

It was further than he thought. He fell on to the hard bags with a frightened grunt.

In an instant there was a key in the door and the guard stood flashing a strong torch. Vincent rolled quietly from the bags. As he lay on top of two metal U-bolts he wanted to cry. He wanted to stand up and say: "Here I am."

Van Dogen couldn't shoot him. Not in cold blood. The whole thing was impossible. It was he, Vincent, who had constructed Van Dogen's original salary. He had invented Van Dogen. He had arranged aeroplanes to fly him through the sky. He had arranged for a gun. He had told Van Dogen to shoot.

Van Dogen walked the aisles of the vast warehouse. It took everything in Vincent to stop himself standing up. "Here I am. I'm a friend." He was like a man who jumps from a tall building because he is frightened of falling from it.

Van Dogen was faceless. A lethal shadow behind a bright light, the formless creature of the very brain that was now sending panic signals to every part of a prickling body.

But Van Dogen noticed nothing. It was simply part of his nightly routine and he left after a couple of minutes.

Vincent lay still for a long time, caught in the sticky webs of his nightmare. When he moved it was because a mouse ran across his shoulder and down his back. He shuddered and jumped back on to the superphosphate. Then although he felt himself already condemned, he moved to the crates of Eupholon. He blinked the torch on for half a second, then off. Another lightning flash. He found them. He took the hateful bottles and filled his shirt pockets and his trouser pockets with them. He didn't know how much to take. He took everything he could fit in.

And now he faced the side door. It was one of four doors. One was the right choice. Two were dangerous. One was deadly. He stood behind the side door and waited. He could hear nothing. No footstep, no breathing, nothing. Slowly, silently, he slid back the latch and waited. Still nothing.

He opened the door and ran. He had been told not to run. He ran straight into Van Dogen who had been standing in front of it.

Vincent shrieked with fear. The shriek came from him without warning, high and piercing, as horrible as a banshee wail. Van

Dogen fell. Vincent fell. The track lay ahead. Vincent was berserk. He kicked Van Dogen's head and threw his rifle against the wall where it went off with a thunderclap.

Half falling, half running, Vincent was on the track down the hill. He tripped, fell, stood and ran. As he tripped the third time he heard a shot and felt a shock in his leg. But he could still run. He felt no pain. In his pockets the broken Eupholon bottles gently sliced his unfeeling skin.

When he woke he was in bed. There was a bandage on his leg and another on his chest. But the first thing he noticed were the three Eupholon bottles standing beside his bed. Beside them, the contents of the five other broken bottles were piled in a little saucer.

The little yellow capsules seemed as precious and beautiful as gold itself. He lay on his bed, laughing.

He balanced the little saucer on his stomach and smiled at the capsules. He took one, not bothering with water. He looked through the open door of the shed to where Solly was digging in the vegetable garden. He took another, impatient for the moment when he would have hands as beautiful as those that now grasped the garden spade.

My revenge lies about me in tatters. Shredded sheets of confusion drift through the air. My story written, but not a story I intended or one my editor will accept.

But I know, if I know anything, that he changed, and I now like him as much as I once despised him.

If I said I was a child, an adolescent, do not take me too literally. Whatever questions you ask of me I have asked myself. We might start with the simplest: has he conned me by helping me prepare my case against him?

It is a possibility. I can't reject it.

Am I reacting to the esteem in which he is held here? When I despised him he was a public joke. Now he is liked. Is this why I like him?

A possibility. I grasp it. It does not sting unduly.

Do I like him because he no longer demands my affection? Do I wish to conquer him now that he has less need of me?

Possibly. But so what?

Do I lack any solid system of values? Is this why I now find blue hands beautiful where once I called them grotesque?

Certainly I have changed. But there must be a functional basis for aesthetics. Blue hands on Upward Island are not blue hands anywhere else.

But then, what of this function? What of the regard blue hands are held in? Should prestige be granted only to the brave? Does physical bravery not suggest a certain lack of imagination? Is it a good qualification for those who will rule?

I don't know.

Is bravery seen to be a masculine virtue? Where are the women with blue hands?

There are none, as yet.

Then am I like a crippled female, applauding male acts of bravado?

No, I am not.

I know only that he walks slowly and talks calmly, is funny without being attention-seeking, accepts praise modestly and is now lying on my bed smiling at me.

I don't move. There is no hurry. But in a moment, sooner or later, I will go over to him and then I will, slowly, carefully, unzip his shorts and there I will see his beautiful blue penis thrusting its aquamarine head upwards towards me. It will be silky, the most curious silkiness imaginable.

I will kneel and take it in my mouth.

If I moan, you will not hear me. What I say, you will never know.

Questions, your questions, will rise like bubbles from deeper water, but I will disregard them, pass them, sinking lower to where there are no questions, nothing but a shimmering searing electric blue.

Exotic Pleasures

1

Lilly Danko had a funny face, but the actual point where one said "this is a funny face" rather than "this is a pretty face" was difficult to establish. Certainly there were little creases around the eyes and small smile lines beside the mouth, yet they had not always been there and she had always had a funny face. It was a long face with a long chin and perhaps it was the slight protuberance of her lower lip that was the key to it, yet it was not pronounced and could be easily overlooked and to make a fuss about it would be to ignore the sparkle in her pale blue eyes. Yet all this is missing the point about faces which are not static things, a blue this, a long that, a collection of little items like clues in a crossword puzzle. For Lillian Danko had a rubber face which squinted its eyes, pursed its lips, wrinkled its nose and expressed, with rare freedom, the humours of its owner.

At the age of eight she had written in a school composition that she wished, when fully grown, to take the profession of clown. And although she had long since forgotten this incident and the cold winter's afternoon on which she had written it, she would not now, at the age of thirty, sitting in a boiling old Chevrolet at the Kennecott Interstellar Space Terminal, have found anything to disown.

Here she was, knitting baby clothes in a beaten-up car while Mort, dressed up in a suit like a travelling salesman, walked the unseen corridors inside the terminal in search of a job as a miner on one of the company's planets, asteroids or moons. She was not likely to share any jokes on the subject with Mort who was stretched as tight as a guitar string about to break. And she wished, as she had found herself wishing more and more lately,

113

that her father had been alive to share the idiocies of the world with.

She would have astonished him with the news, made him laugh and made him furious all at once. Here, she would have said, we have the romance of space and pointed to the burnt ugly hulk of an interstellar cargo ship lowering itself on to the earth like a dirty old hen going down on its nest. Space had yielded no monsters, no martians, no exotic threats or blessings. The ship roaring bad-temperedly on the platform would contain nothing more beautiful than iron ingots, ball-bearings, and a few embittered workers who were lucky enough to have finished their stint in the untidy backyards of space.

It wasn't funny unless you made it funny and Lilly, four months pregnant, with twenty dollars in her purse, a car that needed two hundred dollars and a husband who was fighting against three million unemployed to get a job, had no real choice but to make it funny.

"C'est la bloody guerre," she said, holding up her knitting and reflecting that two hundred miles of dusty roads had not done a lot for the whiteness of the garment.

Fuck it, she thought, it'll have to do.

When the face appeared in the open window by her shoulder she got such a fright she couldn't remember whether she'd said "fuck" out loud or just thought it.

"I beg your pardon," she said to the bombed-out face that grinned crookedly through the window.

"Pardon for what?" He was young and there was something crazy about him. His black eyes looked as sleepy as his voice sounded. He was neglected and overgrown with wild curling black hair falling over his eyes and a bristling beard that was just catching up to an earlier moustache.

"I thought I may have said something."

"If you said something," he said, "I didn't hear it. I am definitely at least half deaf in one ear."

"I probably didn't say it then," she said carefully, wondering if he was going to rob her or if he was just crazy. "Are you looking for a lift?"

"Not me." He stood back from the window so she could see his white overalls with their big Kennecott insignia. He was tall and thin like a renegade basketball player. "This," he gestured laconically to include the whole area of car park, administration building, docking platforms and dry parched earth, "This is my home. So," he paused for a moment as if what he had said had made him inexplicably sad, "so I don't need a lift, thank you."

"Any jobs in there?"

"Let's say there are an awful lot of people in there waiting to be told no."

Lilly nodded. "Yeah, well . . ."

"You want to see something?"

"Well that depends what it is."

He walked smoothly back to a little white cleaner's trolley he had left marooned a few yards from the car and trundled it back whistling like one who carries rare gifts.

"If anyone comes," he whispered, "you're asking me directions, OK?"

"OK."

"This," he reached a large hand into the white cart, "is really something special."

He was not exaggerating. For what he now pushed through the window and on to her lap was the most beautiful bird that Lilly Danko had ever dreamed might be possible, more exquisite and delightful than a bird of paradise, a flamingo, or any of the rare and beautiful species she had ever gazed at in picture books. It was not a large bird, about the size of a very big pigeon, but with a long supple neck and a sleek handsome head from which emerged a strong beak that looked just like mother of pearl. Yet such was the splendour of the bird that she hardly noticed the opaline beauty of the beak, or the remarkable eyes which seemed to have all the colours of the rainbow tucked into a matrix of soft brown. It was the bird's colouring that elicited from her an involuntary cry. For the feathers that ran from its smooth head to its graceful tail were of every blue possibly imaginable. Proud Prussian blue at the head then, beneath a necklace of emerald green, ultramarine and sapphire which gave way to dramatic tail feathers of peacock blue. Its powerful chest revealed viridian hidden like precious jewels in an aquaramine sea.

When she felt the first pulse of pure pleasure she imagined that it originated from the colours themselves and later when she tried to explain this first feeling to Mort she would use the word "swoon", savouring the round smooth strangeness of the word.

"Don't it feel nice when you touch it?"

"Oh, yes."

And even as she answered she realized that it was not the colours that gave such pleasure, but that the feeling was associated with stroking the bird itself. "It's like having your back rubbed."

"Better."

"Yes," she said, "better. It gets you right at the base of the neck."

"It gets you just about everywhere." And something about the way he said it made her realize that he wasn't showing her this bird out of idle interest, but that he was going to offer it for sale. It was an exotic, of course, and had probably been smuggled in by some poor miner looking for an extra buck. If the crew-cut Protestants who had begun the push into space with such obsessive caution had seen the laxness of the space companies with quarantine matters they would have shrieked with horror. But NASA had wilted away and no terrible catastrophe had hit the earth. There were exotic shrubs which needed to be fed extra-terrestrial trace elements to keep them alive, a few dozen strange new weeds of no particular distinction, and a poor small lizardish creature raised for its hallucinogenic skin.

But there had been nothing as strange and beautiful as this and she calculated its value in thousands of dollars. When she was invited to make an offer she reluctantly handed it back, or tried to, because as she held it up to the man he simply backed away.

"You've got to make an offer. You can't not make an offer."

She put the bird, so placid she thought it must be drugged, back on her lap and stroked sadly. "OK. I'll be the bunny. How much do you want?"

He held up two hands.

"Ten dollars?"

"Is that cheap or is it cheap?"

"It's cheap, but I can't."

"You should have made an offer."

"I can't," she said hopelessly, thinking of Mort and what he would say. God knows the world pressed in on him heavily enough. Yet the thrilling thought that she could own such a marvel, that she need never hand it back, crept into her mind and lodged there, snug and comfortable as a child sleeping beneath a soft blanket.

"I can only offer five," she said, thinking that she couldn't offer five at all.

"Done."

"Oh, shit."

"You don't want it?"

"Oh yes, I want it," she said dryly, "you know I want it." She put the bird down on the seat, where it sat waiting for nothing more than to be picked up again, and took five of their precious dollars from her handbag. "Well," she said, handing over the money, "I guess we can always eat it." Then, seeing the shocked look on the wild young face: "Just joking."

"If you don't want it . . ."

"I want it. I want it. What does it eat? Breafast cereal and warm milk?"

"I've got feed for it, so don't sweat."

"And the feed is extra, right?"

"My dear Dolores," he said, "where this bird comes from, the stuff it eats grows on trees. If you'd be nice enough to open the boot I'll give you a bag of it and our transaction, as they say, will be finito."

She opened the boot and he wheeled round his cleaner's trolley and hoisted a polythene sack into the car.

"What do I do when it's eaten all this?"

But he was already gliding across the car park towards the administration building. "Well *then*," he giggled over his shoulder, "you're going to have to *eat* it."

The giggling carried across the hot tarmac and got lost in the heat haze.

Lillian went back to the car and was still stroking the bird when Mort came back.

Through pale veils of pleasure she saw him walking back across the blistering car park and she knew, before he arrived at the car, exactly what his eyes would look like. She had seen those eyes more and more recently, like doors to comfortable and familiar rooms that suddenly open to reveal lift wells full of broken cables. She should have taken him in her arms then and held him, stroked his neck until the lights came back on in those poor defeated eyes, eyes which had once looked at the world with innocent certainty, which had sought nothing more than the contentment of being a good gardener, calm eyes without fear and ambition. She should have taken him in her arms, but she had the bird and she sat there, stroking it stupidly, like someone who won't leave a hot shower until the water goes cold.

He came and sat behind the wheel, not looking at her.

"Take off your coat, honey," she said gently, putting a hand on his. "Come on, take it off."

It was then that he saw the bird.

"What's that?"

Her left hand was still stroking it. She ran a finger down its opaline bill, across its exquisitely smooth head and down its glowing blue back. "It's a bird. Stroke it." She tugged his hand, a hand which each day had become smoother and softer, towards the bird, and the bird, as if understanding, craned its supple neck towards him. "It'll make you feel better."

But Mort put both hands on the steering wheel and she saw his knuckles whiten. She was frightened then. He was a dark well she had only thought of as calm and still, but that was in the easy confidence of employment, in times without threat. Now, when she said what she had to say, something would happen.

"Mort, I'm sorry. I paid five dollars for it. I'm sorry, Mort."

He opened the door and walked slowly around the car. She watched him. He didn't look at her. He walked around the car a second time and she saw his face colouring. Then he started kicking it. He moved slowly, methodically, kicking it every couple of feet as if he wished to leave no part of its dull chalky body unpunished. When he had finished he came and sat down again, resting his head against the wheel.

Lilly got out of the car and walked to the driver's side.

"Come on bugalugs," she said, "move over. I'm driving."

She slid behind the wheel, thinking that in another month she wouldn't be able to fit behind it, and when he moved over she passed him the bird. By the time they had left the terminal he was stroking it. His face had relaxed and resumed its normal quiet innocence and she remembered the days they had worked together as gardeners on the Firestone Estate as if this were some lost Paradise from which they had been inexplicably expelled by a stern fascist god.

"Let's stay in a motel," she said. "Let's have a hot shower and a good meal and get drunk and have a nice fuck in a big bed."

"And be broke in the morning," he said, but smiled.

"One morning we'll be broke. We might as well have fun doing it."

Mort stroked the bird slowly, dreamily.

"Do you like our bird?" she asked.

He smiled. "You're a crazy person, Lilly."

"Do you still love me?"

"Yes," he said, "and I like the bird. Let's have champagne and piss off without paying."

"Champagne it is."

As it turned out, the motel they chose didn't have champagne, but it had an architecture well suited to their plans. Its yellow painted doors faced the highway and when they backed the car into the space in front of the room there was nothing in their way to prevent a fast getaway.

2

Lillian lay on the bed stroking the bird which sat comfortably between her breasts and her swollen belly. The bottle of wine which stood amongst the debris of a meal on the table beside her was very nearly empty.

Mort, his hair wet, sat naked in a chair staring at the television. She envied him his looseness, his easy sexual satisfaction.

"Why don't you put it down," he said.

"In a minute."

"Come and rub my back."

"You're a greedy bugger, Morto."

"You want to be careful with that bird. It probably should have injections or something. You shouldn't fuck around with exotics when you're pregnant."

"You're the only exotic I fuck around with." She looked at

him and thought for the millionth time how pretty he was with his smooth skin and his hard muscles and that beautiful guileless face. "Let's get another bottle." The drunk Mort was more like the old Mort.

Without waiting for an answer she reached over and picked up the phone. She ordered the wine, put the bird in the bathroom with a saucer of seed, threw Mort a pair of trousers and picked up her own dress from where she had dropped it.

It was the manager himself who brought the wine. He wasn't content to hand it through the door. "I'll just pick up the trays," he said and Lilly noted that he already had his foot in the door, like an obnoxious encyclopaedia salesman.

He was a short, slim man, handsome in an over-ripe way, with a mole near his eye and waving dark hair. Lilly didn't like him. She didn't like his highly shined shoes or his neatly pressed flannel trousers. She didn't like the way he looked at the wet towel lying on the floor and the rumpled disordered bed freshly stained from lovemaking.

She sat on the bed while he busied himself with the trays. When she saw he was actually counting the knives and forks she started mimicking him behind his back.

When he announced that a saucer was missing she nearly burst out laughing, as if anyone would pinch one of his stupid tasteless saucers.

"It's in the bathroom," she said and was wondering if she should add, "Where it belongs" when the man took the opportunity to inspect the bathroom.

When he came back he was holding the bird in one hand and the saucer of seed in the other. Lilly took the bird from him and watched him drop the seeds into the rubbish bin.

"There is a house rule against pets. It's quite clearly displayed."

"It's not a pet," she said.

"I can't have people bringing pets here."

She saw Mort put his head in his hands as he anticipated one more setback, one more razor-nick defeat.

She took the saucer from the manager's manicured hand. "Just stroke it," she said, "it has special properties," and smiled inwardly to hear herself use a world like "properties", a leftover from her wasted education.

The manager looked at her with supercilious eyes and was about to give her back the bird when she firmly took hold of his free hand (which he was astonished to find damp with anxiety) and rubbed it down the bird's back. When she took her hand away he continued to stroke it mechanically, the threatened light of authority still shining in his eyes.

"Go on," she encouraged, "it feels nice."

In spite of a private conviction that he was being made a fool of, the manager stroked the bird, at first tentatively and then more surely. The bird, as if understanding the importance of the occasion, brushed its cheek against the manager's and then for a minute or two very little moved in the room but the manager's hand.

Lights from the highway flowed across the wall.

On the television a mute reporter held a microphone towards a weeping man.

Twice Lilly saw the manager trying to give the bird back and twice she saw him fail.

"Feels nice, doesn't it?"

The manager nodded his head and looked embarrassed. She could see that pleasure had made his eyes as gooey as marshmallow.

"Now," she said briskly, holding out her hands for the bird, "I'll put it in the car so we won't be breaking the rules."

"No." He was like a two-year-old with a teddy bear.

"You'll exhaust it," Lilly said, "and we need it for tomorrow. It's our business. That's what I mean about it not being a pet."

"Your business?" the manager asked, and in truth every person in the room was trying to think how this beautiful bird might be anyone's "business".

"It's a Pleasure Bird," Lilly said, lighting a cigarette although she had given them up three months ago. It gave her time to think. "We charge a dollar a minute for people to stroke it."

"You people in show business?"

"Sure am." Lilly exhaled luxuriously and sat down on the bed.

"Dollar a minute, eh. Good work if you can get it." He was being nice now and she allowed herself the luxury of not despising him for it.

"You think that's too expensive?" She held out her arms for the bird. "We've charged more and no one's ever complained."

The manager stepped back from the extended arms, cooing over the bird like a mother keeping its baby from harm.

Lilly started talking. Ideas came to her so fast that she hardly knew how the sentence would end when she started it. "You can have it for half an hour." She watched the manager glow. "In return for the price for this room and the food."

"Done."

"And wine, of course."

"Done."

"For an extra five dollars in cash you can take it to the office so we won't disturb you. We'll get it when time's up."

"Done."

"What's the time, Mort?"

Mort picked up his wristwatch from the top of the mute television. "Nine twenty-three."

"OK, it is now nine twenty-three." She opened the door and ushered the manager out into the night. "I'll pick it up from you at exactly nine fifty-three."

When she shut the door she was grinning so broadly her face hurt. She hugged Mort and said, "I'm a genius. Tell me I'm a genius."

"You're a genius," he said, "but you were crazy to let him take it away."

"Why for Chrissakes?"

"He mightn't give it back."

"Oh fuck, Mort. Stop it."

"I'm sorry, it was just a thought."

"Be positive."

"I am positive."

"Well pour me a glass of wine and tell me I'm beautiful."

The manager had taken the corkscrew and they had to shove the cork in with a pencil.

As it turned out they made an extra twenty dollars cash that night. It was 10.13 before they persuaded the manager to relinquish the bird. They stood in his office holding the wristwatch while the man bought minute after minute of extra time from his petty cash. The phone rang and wasn't answered.

As they left his office, the bird ruffled its feathers and shat on the concrete.

3

Mort didn't want to look at the empty wine bottle or the plan he had agreed to so easily the night before. When Lillian got up he curled himself into a ball and pretended he was still asleep. Lilly knew he wasn't asleep and knew why he was pretending.

"Come on, Mort, don't be chicken shit."

Mort moaned.

"Come on Mort honey or we won't get a stall." She rattled a coffee cup near his ear. "Do you want to get rich or do you want to stay poor? Here's your coffee, baby. It's getting cold."

When Mort finally emerged, tousle-headed and soft as a child's toy, he was in no way prepared for what he saw. Lilly was wearing white overalls and clown's make-up. There were stars round her eyes and padding in her bum.

"Oh Christ, Lilly, please."

"Please what? Drink your coffee."

"Oh shit, please don't. We don't have to do that."

"You heard what I told the man. We're in show business."

"Take it off, please. I don't mind the business with the bird, but we don't have to do all this."

"Drink your coffee and I'll take Charley-boy out for a shit."

When he drove to the markets it was in strained silence. The clown held the bird. The straight man was at the wheel. When the car finally lost its muffler neither of them said anything.

4

The markets had sprung up to meet the needs of the new poor and were supplied and operated by an increasingly sophisticated collection of small-time crooks. The police, by mutual agreement, rarely entered their enclosures and business was thus conducted with some decorum, whether it was the purchase of stolen clothing or illicit drugs (the notorious Lizard Dust was sold here and it was only the poor who tolerated the violent illness that preceded its more pleasant effects). Here you could buy spare parts for rubber thongs, fruit, vegetables, motor cars of questionable origin, poisonous hot dogs and bilious-coloured drinks.

The market they drove to was a vast concrete-paved car park which, at nine o'clock in the morning, was already unpleasantly hot. A blustery wind carried clouds of dust through the stalls, rattled the canvas roofs, and lodged a fine speck of dust in Mort's eye. So it was Lillian who joined the queue for temporary stalls while Mort adjourned, more in embarrassment than pain, to minister to his eye in the men's toilets.

The stall number was 128. It was nothing more than a wooden trestle table with a number painted on the top. Canvas awnings were a luxury they could not yet afford.

Mort stood behind the stall in his suit and tie, red-eyed and sulky. The bird stood stoically on the table. Lilly, resplendent in overalls and clown's face, waddled to and fro in front, a balloon of swollen belly and padded bum.

"It won't work."

"Of course it'll work," she said. But her stomach was a mass of nerves and the baby, probably nervous of the life she had in store for it, kicked irritably inside her. "Don't look like that," she hissed. "I can't do it when you're looking at me like that."

"Do what?"

And she started to do it. She felt a fool. She did badly what she had dreamed would be easy. Her voice sounded high and when she tried to lower it, it came out worse. What she said was hardly impressive and rarely funny. But she began to lumber amongst the crowds clapping her hands and making a fuss.

"See the Pleasure Bird at Stall 128," she yelled. "First three customers get a minute of pleasure for free. Oh yes, oh yes, oh yes. One dollar, one minute. They say it's better than sex. One dollar, one minute and the first three customers get it free."

A crowd of ragged children followed her. She did a cake walk. She danced a waltz with a black man in a pink suit. She fell over a guy-rope and made it look intentional. She attracted a small crowd by the simple device of placing a match box on the ground and making a big show of jumping over it, bowing and smiling when the jump was done. The match box jump was the most successful stunt of all and she gave the laughing crowd the news about stall 128 and the Pleasure Bird.

By the time she'd got lost in an alley of used car parts and been threatened by a woman who was trying to sell bruised apples she was exhausted. She had blisters on her feet from Mort's sandshoes which were four sizes too big and a cut on her hand from the fall over the guy-rope. She limped back to the stall to find an enormous crowd huddled around an old woman who was dreamily stroking the bird. Mort stood beside her with his watch in his hand. The crowd was strangely silent and the woman crooning to the bird seemed vulnerable and rather sad.

"Ten minutes," said Mort.

The woman reluctantly handed the bird back and, from a pocket of her voluminous black dress, produced a half-unravelled blue sock from which she counted out, in notes and coins, ten dollars.

As Mort handed the bird to the next person in the queue, the quiet solemnity of the recipient's face reminded Lilly of a face in her childhood taking communion in a small country church. He was an Italian, a labourer with a blue singlet and dusty boots and he had only had the bird for thirty seconds when he cradled it in one arm and dragged from his pockets a bundle of notes which he placed on the table in a crumpled heap.

"Tell me when time's up," he said, and sat on the trestle table, hunched over the bird, lost in his own private world, impervious to the mutterings of the impatient crowd.

After that they limited the time to three minutes.

They could have worked the market all day but Mort, rather than sharing Lilly's ever increasing sense of triumph, became more and more upset with her costume.

"Take it off. You don't need it now."

"No."

"Please."

"Don't be silly, Mort. It's part of the act."

"You look a fool. I can't stand people laughing at you."

They hissed at each other until one o'clock when Mort, his face red and sullen, suddenly dumped the bird in Lilly's lap and walked away.

At two o'clock she closed the stall and limped painfully back to the car. The bird shat once or twice on the way back, but apart from that seemed none the worse for its handling. Mort didn't seem to have fared so well. He was sitting woodenly inside the boiling car and when she asked him how much he'd taken he simply handed her the money.

She counted two hundred and thirty dollars in notes and didn't bother with the silver.

5

The balcony of their room looked across the wide graceful river which was now silvery and cool in the late light. A rowing eight moved with svelte precision through a canopy of willows and the two black swans descended from the sky above the distant city and Lilly, watching them, imagined the pleasant coolness of the water on their hot bodies.

Her make-up was gone now and she wore a loose white cheese-cloth dress. The ice clinked in her gin and tonic and even the small chink of the glass as it touched the metal filigree table sounded cool and luxurious to her ears. She put her blistered feet up on the railing and stroked the bird gently, letting the pleasure saturate her body.

"Mort."

"Yes."

"You feel OK now?"

He leant across and put his arm on her shoulder. His face was sunburnt and there was a strange red V mark on his chest. He nodded. "Put the bird inside."

"In a minute."

He took his hand back and filled his glass.

Lillian was feeling triumphant. She had a fair idea of the worms that were eating at Mort and she was surprised and a little guilty to discover that she didn't care excessively. She felt cool and rich and amazingly free. After a few minutes she picked up the bird and put it in front of the bathroom mirror where, she discovered, for all its unearthly qualities, it behaved just like a budgerigar.

She went back to the balcony and stood behind Mort, rubbing his broad back and loosening the tense muscles in his neck.

"Tell me I was terrific," she said. "Please say I was great."

Mort hesitated and she felt the muscles under her fingers knot again. "Let's not talk about it now."

She smiled just the same, remembering checking into this hotel, Mort dressed in his salesman's suit, she in her clown's make-up, the bird quietly hidden in a plastic shopping bag.

"Lillian," she said, "you were terrific."

The river was almost black now and, when two birds cut across it towards a certain tree, it was too dark to see the stunning colours by which she might have identified them.

6

Their days were lined with freeways and paved with concrete. They limped south with a boiling radiator and an un-muffled engine. They worked markets, factory gates and even, on one occasion, a forgotten country school where the children let down their tyres to stop them leaving.

Mort no longer complained about the clown, yet his resentment and embarrassment grew like a cancer inside him and he seldom thought of anything else. He had long since stopped touching the Pleasure Bird and the full force of his animosity was beamed towards its small colourful eyes which seemed to contain a universe of malignant intentions.

"God, Jesus, it likes freeways." Lillian held the bird in the air, displaying its ruffled feathers, a signal that it was going to shit.

Mort didn't appear to hear.

"Well stop the car. You're the one who's always worried about where it shits."

Slowly, irritatingly slowly, Mort pulled the car into the white emergency lane and the bird hopped out, shat quickly and effectively, and hopped back in.

"This bird seems intent on spreading shit from one end of Highway 31 to the other."

Mort pulled back on to the road.

"It's really crazy for doing it on nice clean roads. Do you notice that, Morty?"

"Why don't you put it down for a while. You're getting like a bloody junkie."

Lilly said nothing. Her clown's face showed no emotions but

those she had painted on it, and in truth she did not allow herself to think anything of Mort's jealousies. She stroked her index finger slowly down the bird's sensuous back and the slow waves of pleasure blotted out anything else that might have worried her. Even the police siren, when it sounded outside the window, did not startle her. It reached her distantly, having no more importance than a telephone ringing in someone else's dream.

She watched the police car park in front of them and watched the policeman walk back towards their car, pink book in his hand. She heard him talk to Mort about the muffler and saw them both walk around the car looking at the tyres. Even when the policeman stood beside her window and spoke to her she did not think that the words were really addressed to her.

"What sort of bird is that?"

It was only when the question was repeated that she managed to drag her mind to the surface and stare blinking into the strangely young face.

"It's a Pleasure Bird," she smiled, "here." And she passed the passive bird into the big white hands.

"Sure does give a lot of pleasure."

"Sure does."

The bird was passed back and the pink notebook opened.

"Now," he said, "how about we start by you telling me where you got this."

"Why?"

"Because it's an exotic."

"No. It's from New Guinea."

"Look madam, you've chosen the wrong fellow to lay that on. This bird comes from Kennecott 21. I was there two years ."

"Fancy that," said Lilly, "we were told it was from New Guinea."

The notebook closed. "I'll have to take it."

Lilly was struck by the early rumbles of panic. "You can't take it. It's how we earn our living."

But the policeman was already leaning over into the car, his hands ready to engulf the plump jewel-like body.

Then he was suddenly lurching back from the car window with his hands to one eye. Blood streamed down across his knuckles. The bird was pecking at the fingers which covered the other eye. The noise was terrible. She saw Mort running around the car and he was beside her starting the engine, and the bird, as if nothing had happened, was back sitting on her lap.

"Don't go," she said. "Mort. Don't."

But Mort was white with panic and as he accelerated on to the highway Lilly turned helplessly to watch as the policeman staggered blindly on to the road where a giant container truck ran over the top of him.

Even as she watched she stroked the bird in her lap so she had the strange experience of seeing a man killed, of feeling guilt, horror and immeasurable pleasure all at once. The floodgates lifted. Seven colours poured into her brain and mixed into a warm sickly brown mud of emotion.

They turned east down a dusty road which led through the rusting gates of neglected farms. Grass grew through the centre of the road and swished silkily beneath the floor. Lillian began to remove her make-up. Mort, pale and shaken, hissed inaudible curses at the dusty windscreen.

7

Yet their life did not stop, but limped tiredly on through a series of markets and motel rooms and if their dreams were now marred by guilt and echoes, neither mentioned it to the other.

They bought a small radio and listened to the news, but nothing was ever said about the policeman and Lilly was shocked to find herself hoping that his head had been crushed, obliterating the evidence of the attack.

Mort drew away from her more and more, as if the crime had been hers and hers alone. When he spoke, his sentences were as cold and utilitarian as three-inch nails.

He took to calling the bird "the little murderer". There was something chilling in the way that dreamy childlike face moved its soft lips and said such things as: "Have you fed the little murderer?"

He was filled with anger and resentment and fear which had so many sources he himself didn't know where the rivers of his pain began, from which wells they drew, from which fissures they seeped.

He watched Lillian perform at the markets, saw the bird shit on every hard surface that came its way, and he watched it narrowly, warily, and on more than one occasion thought he saw the bird watching him. Once, removing the bird from bedroom to bathroom for the night against Lilly's will, he thought that the bird had burned him.

At the markets he did less and less and now it was Lilly who not only attracted the crowds but also took the money and kept time. He felt useless and hopeless, angry at himself that he was too stiff and unbending to do the things that he should to earn a living, resentful that his wife could do it all without appearing to try, angry that she should accept his withdrawal so readily, angry that she showed no guilt or remorse about a man's death, angry when she met his silences with her own, angry that he who hated the bird should continue to want the money it brought him.

They spent three hundred dollars on the car. Its radiator no longer boiled. A shiny new muffler was bolted securely into place. Yet the sight of that clean metal exhaust pipe sticking out from beneath the rear bumper made him close his eyes and suck in his breath.

He drank champagne without pleasure and made love with silent rage while Lilly's eyes followed invisible road maps on the ceiling.

With sticky tissues still between her legs she brought the bird to bed and stroked it till she drifted into sleep. Even the ease of her sleep enraged him, giving him further proof of her cold self-sufficiency.

And it was on one such night, with his wife asleep on the twin bed beside him, with a cheap air-conditioner rattling above his head, that he saw the current affairs bulletin on the latest quarantine breakdown. He watched it without alarm or even any particular interest. There had been many such breakdowns before and there would be many again in the future. As usual there were experts who were already crying catastrophe, and these were, of course, balanced by optimists who saw no serious threat to the terrestrial environment.

The breakdown in this case involved a tree, named by journalists as the Kennecott Rock-drill. The seeds of this tree took to their new home with a particular enthusiasm. Adapted for a harsh, rocky environment the seeds had a very specialized survival mechanism. Whereas a terrestrial seed secreted mucus, the Kennecott Rock-drill secreted a strong acid much as a lichen did. When dropped on the rocky surfaces of its home planet the secreted acid produced a small hole. In this self-made bed the root tips expanded, using osmosis, and little by little cracked the rock, pushing a strong and complicated root system down a quarter of a mile if need be. In a terrestrial environment the whole process was speeded up, moisture and a less formidable ground surface accelerating the growth rate to such an extent that a single seed could emerge as a small tree on a busy freeway in less than seven days.

Mort watched the programme with the same detachment with which earlier generations had greeted oil spills or explosions in chemical plants.

Service stations in the north were overcome by green vegetation. Men in masks sprayed poisons which proved ineffective. People lay in hospital beds seriously ill from drinking water contaminated by this same herbicide. Fire, it seemed, rather than slowing the spread of the Rock-drill merely accelerated the germination of the seeds. Mort watched an overgrown house sacrificed to fire and then the result, a week later, when giant Rock-drills grew in the burnt-out ruins. He would have turned complacently to the late movie on another channel, had they not shown films of the Rock-drill's home environment.

There he watched the strange rocky outcrops of a Kennecott planet, saw the miners working beneath a merciless sun and silently thanked god he had not succeeded in getting a job there. He admired the beauty of the giant trees silhouetted against a purple sunset and then, sitting up with a cry of recognition, saw the blocks of birds that crowded the gnarled branches.

The birds were identical to the one which sat silently on the end of Lilly's bed.

He sat shaking his head, as puzzled and secretly pleased as any lost citizen who finds his hated neighbour on public television.

8

The argument started the next morning at breakfast and flickered and flared for the next two days as they pursued an even more erratic course, dictated more by Mort's perversity than the location of markets. His eyes blazed, bright, righteous and triumphant. A strange pallor lay like a sheet across his tucked-in face.

To Lilly he became a mosquito buzzing on the edges of an otherwise contented sleep. She slapped at the mosquito and wished it would go away. The bird, now officially outlawed for its role in spreading the Rock-drill seed, sat contentedly in her lap as she stroked it. The stroking rarely stopped now. It was as if she wanted nothing more from life than to stroke its blue jewelled back for ever and it seemed, for the bird, the arrangement was perfect.

"Are you listening to me?"

"Yes." She hadn't been.

"We'll have to hand it in."

"No we won't." There was no anger in her voice.

Mort sucked in breath through clenched teeth.

She heard the intake of air but it caused her no concern. No matter how he shouted or hissed, no matter what he said about the bird, there was only one danger to Mort and it had nothing to do with quarantine breakdowns. From the depths of the blue well she now lived in, Lilly acknowledged the threat posed by the Kennecott Rock-drill and in her mind she had fulfilled her obligation to the world by collecting the bird's shit in a cardboard box. It was as simple as that. As for the potential violence of the bird, she saw no problem in that either. It was only violent when it was threatened. It was wiser not to threaten it.

These simple answers to the problems did not satisfy Mort and she concluded, correctly, that there must be other things which threatened him more directly.

"Do you know why you want me to get rid of this bird?" she said.

"Of course I bloody know."

"I don't think you do."

"All right," he said slowly, "you tell me."

"First, you don't like the bird because you hate to see me being able to earn a living. Then you hate yourself because you can't. You're so fucked-up you can't see I'm doing it for both of us."

"Bullshit."

"No, Morty. Not bullshit, fact. But most of all," she paused, wondering if it was wise to say all this while he was driving.

"Yes, most of all . . ."

"Most of all it is because you're frightened of pleasure. You can't have pleasure yourself. You don't know how. You can't stand the sight of me having pleasure. You can't give me pleasure, so you're damned if anything else is going to."

The car swung off the road and on to the verge. It skidded in gravel. For a moment, as the wheels locked and the car slid sideways, she thought that it would roll. It turned 180 degrees and faced back the way it had come, its engine silent, red lights burning brightly on the dash.

"You're saying I'm a lousy fuck."

"I'm saying you give me no pleasure."

"You used to make enough noise."

"I loved you. I wanted to make you happy."

Mort didn't say anything for a moment. The silence was a tight pink membrane stretched through pale air.

She looked at the warning lights, thinking the ignition should be turned off.

She was expecting something, but when the blow came she did not know what happened. It felt like an ugly granite lump of hate, not a fist. Her head was hit sideways against the window.

Everything that happened then was slow and fast all at once. She felt wetness on her face and found tears rather than the blood she had expected. At the same time she saw the bird rise from her lap and fly at Mort. She saw Mort cower beneath the steering wheel and saw the bird peck at his head. She saw, like a slow motion replay, the policeman walk on to the road howling with pain. She quietly picked up the bird in both hands as she had done it a hundred times every day and quietly wrung its neck.

She held the body on her lap, stroking it.

She watched Mort whom she did not love weep across the steering wheel.

They drove in grey silence for there was nothing else to do. It was as if they travelled along the bottom of the ocean floor. If there was sun they didn't see it. If there were clouds they took no note of their shapes or colours.

If they had come to a motel first it is possible that the ending might have been different but, turning down a road marked A34, they came to their first forest of Kennecott Rock-drill. It grew across the road like a wall. It spread through a shopping complex and across a service station. Water gushed from broken pipes.

When they left the car the smell of gasoline enveloped them and in the service station they saw a huge underground tank pushed up through a tangle of roots and broken concrete, its ruptured skin veiled by an inflammable haze.

Lilly heard a sharp noise, a drumming, and looked to see Mort hammering on the car's bonnet with clenched fists, drumming like a child in a tantrum. He began screaming. There were no words at first. And then she saw what he had seen. Above their heads the branches of the trees were crowded with the birds, each one as blue and jewel-like as the dead body that lay in the front seat of the car. Through mists of gasoline Lilly saw, or imagined she saw, a curious arrogance in their movements, for all the world like troops who have just accomplished a complicated and elegant victory.

The Last Days of a Famous Mime

1

The Mime arrived on Alitalia with very little luggage: a brown paper parcel and what looked like a woman's handbag.

Asked the contents of the brown paper parcel he said, "String."

Asked what the string was for he replied: "Tying up bigger parcels."

It had not been intended as a joke, but the Mime was pleased when the reporters laughed. Inducing laughter was not his forte. He was famous for terror.

Although his state of despair was famous throughout Europe, few guessed at his hope for the future. "The string," he explained, "is a prayer that I am always praying."

Reluctantly he untied his parcel and showed them the string. It was blue and when extended measured exactly fifty-three metres.

The Mime and the string appeared on the front pages of the evening papers.

2

The first audiences panicked easily. They had not been prepared for his ability to mime terror. They fled their seats continually. Only to return again.

Like snorkel divers they appeared at the doors outside the concert hall with red faces and were puzzled to find the world as they had left it.

3

Books had been written about him. He was the subject of an award-winning film. But in his first morning in a provincial town he was distressed to find that his performance had not been liked by the one newspaper's one critic.

"I cannot see," the critic wrote, "the use of invoking terror in an audience."

The Mime sat on his bed, pondering ways to make his performance more light-hearted.

4

As usual he attracted women who wished to still the raging storms of his heart.

They attended his bed like highly paid surgeons operating on a difficult case. They were both passionate and intelligent. They did not suffer defeat lightly.

5

Wrongly accused of merely miming love in his private life he was somewhat surprised to be confronted with hatred.

"Surely," he said, "if you now hate me, it was you who were imitating love, not I."

"You always were a slimy bastard," she said. "What's in that parcel?"

"I told you before," he said helplessly, "string."

"You're a liar," she said.

But later when he untied the parcel he found that she had opened it to check on his story. Her understanding of the string had been perfect. She had cut it into small pieces like spaghetti in a lousy restaurant.

6

Against the advice of the tour organizers he devoted two concerts entirely to love and laughter. They were disasters. It was felt that love and laughter were not, in his case, as instructive as terror.

The next performance was quickly announced.

TWO HOURS OF REGRET.

Tickets sold quickly. He began with a brief interpretation of love using it merely as a prelude to regret which he elaborated on in a complex and moving performance which left the audience pale and shaken. In a final flourish he passed from regret to loneliness to terror. The audience devoured the terror like brave tourists eating the hottest curry in an Indian restaurant.

7

"What you are doing," she said, "is capitalizing on your neuroses. Personally I find it disgusting, like someone exhibiting their club foot, or Turkish beggars with strange deformities."

He said nothing. He was mildly annoyed at her presumption: that he had not thought this many, many times before.

With perfect misunderstanding she interpreted his passivity as disdain.

Wishing to hurt him, she slapped his face.

Wishing to hurt her, he smiled brilliantly.

8

The story of the blue string touched the public imagination. Small brown paper packages were sold at the doors of his concerts.

Standing on stage he could hear the packages being noisily unwrapped. He thought of American matrons buying Muslim prayer rugs.

9

Exhausted and weakened by the heavy schedule he fell prey to the doubts that had pricked at him insistently for years. He lost all sense of direction and spent many listless hours by himself, sitting in a motel room listening to the air-conditioner.

He had lost confidence in the social uses of controlled terror. He no longer understood the audience's need to experience the very things he so desperately wished to escape from.

He emptied the ashtrays fastidiously.

He opened his brown paper parcel and threw the small pieces of string down the cistern. When the torrent of white water subsided they remained floating there like flotsam from a disaster at sea.

10

The Mime called a press conference to announce that there would be no more concerts. He seemed small and foreign and smelt of garlic. The press regarded him without enthusiasm. He watched their hovering pens anxiously, unsuccessfully willing them to write down his words.

Briefly he announced that he wished to throw his talent open to broader influences. His skills would be at the disposal of the people, who would be free to request his services for any purpose at any time.

His skin seemed sallow but his eyes seemed as bright as those on a nodding fur mascot on the back window ledge of an American car.

11

Asked to describe death he busied himself taking Polaroid photographs of his questioners.

12

Asked to describe marriage he handed out small cheap mirrors with MADE IN TUNISIA written on the back.

13

His popularity declined. It was felt that he had become obscure and beyond the understanding of ordinary people. In response he requested easier questions. He held back nothing of himself in his effort to please his audience.

14

Asked to describe an aeroplane he flew three times around the city, only injuring himself slightly on landing.

15

Asked to describe a river, he drowned himself.

16

It is unfortunate that this, his last and least typical performance, is the only one which has been recorded on film.

There is a small crowd by the river bank, no more than thirty people. A small, neat man dressed in a grey suit picks his way through some children who seem more interested in the large plastic toy dog they are playing with.

He steps into the river, which, at the bank, is already quite deep. His head is only visible above the water for a second or two. And then he is gone.

A policeman looks expectantly over the edge, as if waiting for him to reappear. Then the film stops.

Watching this last performance it is difficult to imagine how this man stirred such emotions in the hearts of those who saw him.

A Windmill in the West

The soldier has been on the line for two weeks. No one has come. The electrified fence stretches across the desert, north to south, south to north, going as far as the eye can see without bending or altering course. In the heat its distant sections shimmer and float. Only at dusk do they return to their true positions. With the exception of the break at the soldier's post the ten foot high electrified fence is uninterrupted. Although, further up the line, perhaps twenty miles along, there may be another post similar or identical to this one. Perhaps there is not. Perhaps the break at this post is the only entry point, the only exit point—no one has told him. No one has told him anything except that he must not ask questions. The officer who briefed him told the soldier only what was considered necessary: that the area to the west could be considered the United States, although in fact, it was not; that the area to the east of the line could be considered to be Australia, which it was; that no one, with the exception of U.S. military personnel carrying a special pass from Southern Command, should be permitted to cross the line at this point. They gave him a photostat copy of an old pass, dated two years before, and drove him out to the line in a Ford truck. That was all.

No one in the United States had briefed him about the line—its existence was never mentioned. No one anywhere has told him if the line is part of a large circle, or whether it is straight; no one has taken the trouble to mention the actual length of the line. The line may go straight across Australia, for all the soldier knows, from north to south, cutting the country in half. And, even if this were the case, he would not know where, would not be able to point out the line's location on a map. He was flown from the United States, together with two cooks, five jeeps, and various other supplies, directly to the base at Yallamby. After they landed there was no orientation brief, no maps—he waited fifteen hours before someone came to claim him.

So, for all he knows, this line could be anywhere in Australia. It is even possible that there are two parallel lines, or perhaps several hundred, each at thirty-mile intervals. It is even possible that some lines are better than others, that not all of them stretch through this desert with its whining silence and singing in the line.

The road crosses the line, roughly, at a right angle. The fact that it is not exactly a right angle has caused him considerable irritation for two weeks. For the first week he was unable to locate the thing that was irritating him, it was something small and hard, like a stone in his boot.

The bitumen road crosses the line at the slightest angle away from a right angle. He has calculated it to be, approximately, eighty-seven degrees. In another month those missing three degrees could become worse.

The soldier, who is standing on double white lines that run the length of the road, kicks a small red rock back into the desert.

The soldier sits inside the door of the caravan, his eyes focused on the dusty screen of his dark glasses, his long body cradled in his armchair. He was informed, three weeks ago, that he would be permitted to bring a crate of specified size containing personal effects. From this he gathered some ill-defined idea of what was ahead of him. He is not a young soldier, and remembering other times in other countries he located an armchair that would fit within the specified dimensions. The remaining space he packed with magazines, thrillers, and a copy of the Bible. The Bible was an afterthought. It puzzled him at the time, but he hasn't thought of it or looked at it since.

He had expected, while he put the crate together, that he would have a fight on his hands, sooner or later, because of that armchair. Because he had envisaged a camp. But there was no camp, merely this caravan on the line.

The soldier polishes and cleans his dark glasses, which were made to prescription in Dallas, Texas, and stands up inside the caravan. As usual he bumps his head. His natural stoop has become more exaggerated, more protective, because of this caravan. He has hit his head so often that he now has a permanent patch that is red and raw, just at the top, just where the crewcut is thin and worn like an old sandy carpet.

But this is not a caravan, not a real caravan. It resembles an aluminium coffin, an aluminium coffin with a peculiar swivelling base constructed like the base of a heavy gun. The soldier has no idea why anyone should design it that way, but he has taken advantage of it, changing the direction of the caravan so that the front door faces away from the wind. Changing the view, is what he calls it, changing the view.

No matter which way you point that door the view doesn't alter. All that changes is the amount of fence you see. Because there is nothing else—no mountains, no grass, nothing but a windmill on the western side of the line. The corporal who drove him out in the Ford said that things grew in the desert if it rained. The corporal said that it rained two years ago. He said small flowers grew all over the desert, flowers and grass.

Once or twice the soldier has set out to walk to the windmill, for no good reason. He is not curious about its purpose—it is like the road, an irritation.

He took plenty of ammunition, two grenades, and his carbine, and while he walked across the hot rocky desert he kept an eye on the caravan and the break in the wire where the road came through. He was overcome with tiredness before he reached the windmill, possibly because it was further away than it appeared to be, possibly because he knew what it would look like when he got there.

The day before yesterday he came close enough to hear it clanking, a peculiar metallic noise that travelled from the windmill to him, across the desert. No one else in the world could hear that clanking. He spat on the ground and watched his spittle disappear. Then he fired several rounds in the direction of the windmill, just on semi-automatic. Then he turned around and walked slowly back, his neck prickling.

The thermometer recorded 120 degrees inside the caravan when he got back.

The walls are well insulated—about one foot and three inches in thickness. But he has the need to have the door open and the air-conditioner became strange and, eventually, stopped. He hasn't reported the breakdown because it is, after all, his own making. And, even if they came out from Yallamby and fixed it, he would leave the door open again and it would break down again. And there would be arguments about the door.

He needs the air. It is something he has had since he was small, the need for air coming from outside. Without good air he has headaches, and the air-conditioner does not give good air. Perhaps the other soldiers at the other posts along the line sit inside and peer at the desert through their thick glass windows, if there are any other soldiers. But it is not possible for him to do that. He likes to have the air.

He has had the need since he was a child and the need has not diminished so that now, in his forty-third year, the fights he has fought to keep windows open have brought him a small degree of fame. He is tall and thin and not born to be a fighter, but his need for air forced him to learn. He is not a straight fighter, and would be called dirty in many places, but he has the ability to win, and that is all he has ever needed.

Soon he will go out and get himself another bucket of scorpions. The method is simple in the extreme. There are holes every two or three inches apart, all the way across the desert. If you pour water down these holes the scorpions come up. It amuses him to think that they come up to drink. He laughs quietly to himself and talks to the scorpions as they emerge. When they come up he scoops them into a coffee mug and tips them into the blue bucket. Later on he pours boiling water from the artesian bore over the lot of them. That is how he fills a bucket with scorpions.

To the north of the road he marked out a rough grid. Each square of this grid (its interstices marked with empty bottles and beer cans) can be calculated to contain approximately one bucket of scorpions. His plan, a new plan, developed only yesterday, is to rid the desert of a bucket full for each day he is here. As of this moment one square can be reckoned to be clear of scorpions.

The soldier, who has been sitting in his armchair, pulls on his heavy boots and goes in search of yesterday's bucket. The glare outside the caravan is considerable, and, in spite of the sunglasses, he needs to shade his eyes. Most of the glare comes from the aluminium caravan. Everything looks like one of those colour photographs he took in Washington, over-exposed and bleached out.

The blue bucket is where he put it last night, beside the generator. Not having to support the air-conditioning, the generator has become quiet, almost silent.

He takes the blue bucket which once held strawberry jam and empties a soft black mass of scorpions on to the road, right in the middle, across those double white lines. In another two weeks he will have fifteen neat piles right along the centre of the road. If you could manage two bucketfuls a day there would be thirty. Perhaps, if he became really interested in it and worked hard at it, he could have several hundred buckets of scorpions lined up along those double lines. But sooner or later he will be relieved from duty or be visited by the supply truck, and then he will have to remove the scorpions before the truck reaches the spot.

He walks slowly, his boots scuffing the road, the blue bucket banging softly against his long leg, and enters the caravan where he begins to search for a coffee mug. Soon he will go out and get himself another bucket of scorpions.

The sun is low now and everything is becoming quieter, or perhaps it is only that the wind, the new wind, suggests quietness while being, in fact, louder. The sand which lies on the hard rocky base of the desert is swept in sudden gusts and flurries. Occasionally one of these small storms engulfs him, stinging his face and arms. But for all the noises of sand and wind it appears to him that there is no sound at all.

He stands in the middle of the road, his shoulders drooping, a copy of *Playboy* in his hand, and gazes along the road, as far as he can see. Somewhere up towards the western horizon he can make out an animal of some type crossing the road. It is not a kangaroo. It is something else but he doesn't know exactly what.

He gazes to the west, over past the windmill, watching the slowly darkening sky. Without turning his legs he twists his trunk and head around to watch the sun sinking slowly in the eastern sky.

He squats a little, bending just enough to place the copy of

Playboy gently on the road. Walking slowly towards the caravan he looks once more at the windmill which is slowly disappearing in the dark western sky.

The carbine is lying on his bunk. He clips a fresh magazine into it, and returns to his place on the road, his long legs moving slowly over the sand, unhurriedly. The noise of his boots on the roadway reminds him of countless parades. He flicks the carbine to automatic and, having raised it gently to his shoulder, pours the whole magazine into the sun which continues to set to the east.

He lies on the bunk in the hot darkness wearing only his shorts and a pair of soft white socks. He has always kept a supply of these socks, a special type purchased from Fish & Degenhardt in Dallas, thick white socks with heavy towelling along the sole to soak up the sweat. He bought a dozen pairs from Fish & Degenhardt three weeks ago. They cost $4.20 a pair.

He lies on the bunk and listens to the wind in the fence.

There are some things he must settle in his mind but he would prefer, for the moment, to forget about them. He would like not to think about east or west. What is east and what is west could be settled quickly and easily. There is an army issue compass on the shelf above his head. He could go outside now, take a flashlight with him, and settle it.

But now he is unsure as to what he has misunderstood. Perhaps the area to the geographical east is to be considered as part of the United States, and the area to the west as Australian. Or perhaps it is as he remembered: the west is the United States and the east Australian; perhaps it is this and he has simply misunderstood which was east and which west. He was sure that the windmill was in the United States. He seems to remember the corporal making some joke about it, but it is possible that he misunderstood the joke.

There is also another possibility concerning the sun setting in the east. It creeps into his mind from time to time and he attempts to prevent it by blocking his ears.

He has been instructed to keep intruders on the outside but he is no longer clear as to what "outside" could mean. If they had taken the trouble to inform him of what lay "inside" he would be able to evaluate the seriousness of his position. He considers telephoning the base to ask, and dismisses it quickly, his neck and ears reddening at the thought of it.

It is hot, very hot. He tries to see the *Playboy* nude in the dark, craning his head up from the pillow. He runs his dry fingers over the shiny paper and thinks about the line. If only they had told him if it was part of a circle, or a square, or whatever shape it was. Somehow that could help. It would not be so bad if he knew the shape.

Now, in the darkness, it is merely a line, stretching across the desert as far as his mind can see. He pulls his knees up to his stomach, clutching his soft socks in his big dry hands, and rolls over on his side.

Outside the wind seems to have stopped. Sometimes he thinks he can hear the windmill clanking.

The alarm goes at 4.30 a.m. and, although he wakes instantly, his head is still filled with unravelled dreams. He does not like to remember those dreams. A long line of silk thread spun out of his navel, and he, the spinner, could not halt the spinning. He can still taste the emptiness in his stomach. It is not the emptiness of hunger but something more, as if the silk has taken something precious from him.

He bumps around the caravan in the dark. He does not like to use the light. He did not use it last night either. He is happier in the dark. He spills a bottle of insect repellant but finds the coffee next to it. With his cigarette lighter he lights the primus.

He could go outside if he wanted, and take boiling water straight from the artesian bore, but he is happier to boil it. It makes a small happy noise inside the caravan which is normally so dense and quiet, like a room in an expensive hotel.

It will become light soon. The sun will rise but he doesn't think about this, about the sun, about the line, about what the line divides, encircles, or contains, about anything but the sound of boiling water.

The blue flame of the primus casts a flickering light over the pits and hollows of his face. He can see his face in the shaving mirror, like the surface of a planet, a photograph of the surface of the moon in *Life* magazine. It is strange and unknown to him. He rubs his hands over it, more to cover the reflected image than to feel its texture.

The coffee is ready now and he dresses while it cools off. For some reason he puts on his dress uniform. Just for a change, is what he tells himself. The uniform is clean and pressed, lying in the bottom of his duffle bag. It was pressed in Dallas Texas and still smells of American starch and the clean steam of those big hot laundries with their automatic presses.

In the middle of the desert the smell is like an old snapshot. He smiles in soft surprise as he puts it on.

He stands in the middle of the road. It is still cold and he stamps up and down looking at the place where the horizon is. He can make nothing out, nothing but stars, stars he is unfamiliar with. He could never memorize them anyway, never remember which was the bear or the bull, and it had caused him no inconvenience, this lack of knowledge.

He stands in the middle of the road and turns his head slowly around, scanning the soft horizon. Sooner or later there will be a patch, lighter than any other, as if a small city has appeared just over the edge, a city with its lights on. Then it will get hot, and before that he will have settled one of the questions concerning east and west.

He turns towards the east. He looks down the road in the direction he has known as "east" for two weeks, for two weeks until he was crazy enough to watch the sun set. He watches now for a long time. He stands still with his hands behind his back, as if bound, and feels a prickling along the back of his neck.

He stands on the road with his feet astride the double white line, in the at-ease position. He remains standing there until an undeniable shadow is cast in front of him. It is his own shadow, long and lean, stretching along the road, cast by the sun which is rising in the "west". He slowly turns to watch the windmill which is silhouetted against the clear morning sky.

It is some time later, perhaps five minutes, perhaps thirty, when he notices the small aeroplane. It is travelling down from the "north", directly above the wire and very low. It occurs to him that the plane is too low to be picked up by radar, but he is not alarmed. In all likelihood it is an inspection tour, a routine check, or even a supply visit. The plane has been to the other posts up "north", a little further along the line.

Only when the plane is very close does he realize that it is civilian. Then it is over him, over the caravan, and he can see its civilian registration. As it circles and comes in to land on the road he is running hard for the caravan and his carbine. He stuffs his pockets full of clips and emerges as the plane comes to rest some ten yards from the caravan.

What now follows, he experiences distantly. As if he himself were observing his actions. He was once in a car accident in California where his tyre blew on the highway. He still remembers watching himself battle to control the car, he watched quite calmly, without fear.

Now he motions the pilot out of the plane and indicates that he should stand by the wing with his hands above his head. Accustomed to service in foreign countries he has no need of the English language. He grunts in a certain manner, waving and poking with the carbine to add meaning to the sounds. The pilot speaks but the soldier has no need to listen.

The pilot is a middle-aged man with a fat stomach. He is dressed in white: shorts, shirt and socks. He has the brown shoes and white skin of a city man. He appears concerned. The soldier cannot be worried by this. He asks the pilot what he wants, using simple English, easy words to understand.

The man replies hurriedly, explaining that he was lost and nearly out of petrol. He is on his way to a mission station, at a place that the soldier does not even bother to hear—it would mean nothing.

The soldier then indicates that the pilot may sit in the shade beneath the wing of the aircraft. The pilot appears doubtful, perhaps thinking of his white clothing, but having looked at the soldier he moves awkwardly under the wing, huddling strangely.

The soldier then explains that he will telephone. He also explains that, should the man try to move or escape, he will be shot.

★

He dials the number he has never dialled before. At the moment of dialling he realizes that he is unsure of what the telephone is connected to: Yallamby base which is on the "outside", or whatever is on the "inside".

The phone is answered. It is an officer, a major he has never heard of. He explains the situation to the major who asks him details about the type of fuel required. The soldier steps outside and obtains the information, then returns to the major on the phone.

Before hanging up the major asks, what side of the wire was he on?

The soldier replies, on the outside.

It is two hours before the truck comes. It is driven by a captain. That is strange, but it does not surprise the soldier. However it disappoints him, for he had hoped to settle a few questions regarding the "outside" and "inside". It will be impossible to settle them now.

There are few words. The captain and the soldier unload several drums and a handpump. The captain reprimands the soldier for his lack of courtesy to the pilot. The soldier salutes.

The captain and the pilot exchange a few words while the soldier fixes the tailboard of the truck—the pilot appears to be asking questions but it is impossible to hear what he asks or how he is answered.

The captain turns the truck around, driving off the road and over the scorpion grid, and returns slowly to wherever he came from.

The pilot waves from his open cockpit. The soldier returns his greeting, waving slowly from his position beside the road. The pilot guns the motor and taxis along the road, then turns, ready for take-off.

At this point it occurs to the soldier that the man may be about to fly across the "inside", across what is the United States. It is his job to prevent this. He tries to wave the man down but he seems to be occupied with other things, or misunderstands the waving. The plane is now accelerating and coming towards the soldier. He runs toward it, waving.

It is impossible to know which is the "inside". It would have been impossible to ask a captain. They could have court-martialled him for that.

He stands beside the road as the small plane comes towards him, already off the road. It is perhaps six feet off the road when he levels his carbine and shoots. The wings tip slightly to the left and then to the right. In the area known as the "west" the small aeroplane tips on to its left wing, rolls, and explodes in a sudden blast of flame and smoke.

The soldier, who is now standing in the middle of the road, watches it burn.

He has a mattock, pick, and shovel. He flattens what he can and breaks those members that can be broken. Then he begins to dig a hole in which to bury the remains of the aeroplane. The ground is hard, composed mostly of rock. He will need a big hole. His uniform, his dress uniform, has become blackened and dirty. He digs continually, his fingers and hands bleeding and blistered. There are many scorpions. He cannot be bothered with them, there is no time. He tells them, there is no time now.

It is hot, very hot.

He digs slowly with fatigue.

Sometimes, while he digs, he thinks he can hear the windmill clanking, and wonders if the windmill *could* possibly hear him.

American Dreams

No one can, to this day, remember what it was we did to offend him. Dyer the butcher remembers a day when he gave him the wrong meat and another day when he served someone else first by mistake. Often when Dyer gets drunk he recalls this day and curses himself for his foolishness. But no one seriously believes that it was Dyer who offended him.

But one of us did something. We slighted him terribly in some way, this small meek man with the rimless glasses and neat suit who used to smile so nicely at us all. We thought, I suppose, he was a bit of a fool and sometimes he was so quiet and grey that we ignored him, forgetting he was there at all.

When I was a boy I often stole apples from the trees at his house up in Mason's Lane. He often saw me. No, that's not correct. Let me say I often sensed that he saw me. I sensed him peering out from behind the lace curtains of his house. And I was not the only one. Many of us came to take his apples, alone and in groups, and it is possible that he chose to exact payment for all these apples in his own peculiar way.

Yet I am sure it wasn't the apples.

What has happened is that we all, all eight hundred of us, have come to remember small transgressions against Mr. Gleason who once lived amongst us.

My father, who has never borne malice against a single living creature, still believes that Gleason meant to do us well, that he loved the town more than any of us. My father says we have treated the town badly in our minds. We have used it, this little valley, as nothing more than a stopping place. Somewhere on the way to somewhere else. Even those of us who have been here many years have never taken the town seriously. Oh yes, the place is pretty. The hills are green and the woods thick. The stream is full of fish. But it is not where we would rather be.

For years we have watched the films at the Roxy and dreamed, if not of America, then at least of our capital city. For our own town, my father says, we have nothing but contempt. We have treated it badly, like a whore. We have cut down the giant shady trees in the main street to make doors for the school house and seats for the football pavilion. We have left big holes all over the countryside from which we have taken brown coal and given back nothing.

The commercial travellers who buy fish and chips at George the Greek's care for us more than we do, because we all have dreams of the big city, of wealth, of modern houses, of big motor cars: American Dreams, my father has called them.

Although my father ran a petrol station he was also an inventor. He sat in his office all day drawing strange pieces of equipment on the back of delivery dockets. Every spare piece of paper in the house was covered with these little drawings and my mother would always be very careful about throwing away any piece of paper no matter how small. She would look on both sides of any piece of paper very carefully and always preserved any that had so much as a pencil mark.

I think it was because of this that my father felt that he understood Gleason. He never said as much, but he inferred that he understood Gleason because he, too, was concerned with similar problems. My father was working on plans for a giant gravel crusher, but occasionally he would become distracted and become interested in something else.

There was, for instance, the time when Dyer the butcher bought a new bicycle with gears, and for a while my father talked of nothing else but the gears. Often I would see him across the road squatting down beside Dyer's bicycle as if he were talking to it.

We all rode bicycles because we didn't have the money for anything better. My father did have an old Chev truck, but he rarely used it and it occurs to me now that it might have had some mechanical problem that was impossible to solve, or perhaps it was just that he was saving it, not wishing to wear it out all at once. Normally, he went everywhere on his bicycle and, when I was younger, he carried me on the cross bar, both of us dismounting to trudge up the hills that led into and out of the main street. It was a common sight in our town to see people pushing bicycles. They were as much a burden as a means of transport.

Gleason also had his bicycle and every lunchtime he pushed and pedalled it home from the shire offices to his little weatherboard house out at Mason's Lane. It was a three-mile ride and people said that he went home for lunch because he was fussy and wouldn't eat either his wife's sandwiches or the hot meal available at Mrs Lessing's café.

But while Gleason pedalled and pushed his bicycle to and from the shire offices everything in our town proceeded as normal. It was only when he retired that things began to go wrong.

Because it was then that Mr Gleason started supervising the building of the wall around the two-acre plot up on Bald Hill. He paid too much for this land. He bought it from Johnny Weeks, who now, I am sure, believes the whole episode was his fault, firstly for cheating Gleason, secondly for selling him the land at all. But Gleason hired some Chinese and set to work to build his wall. It was then that we knew that we'd offended him. My father rode all the way out to Bald Hill and tried to talk Mr Gleason out of his wall. He said there was no need for us to build walls. That no one wished to spy on Mr Gleason or whatever he wished to do on Bald Hill. He said no one was in the least bit interested in Mr Gleason. Mr Gleason, neat in a new sportscoat, polished his glasses and smiled vaguely at his feet. Bicycling back, my father thought that he had gone too far. Of course we had an interest in Mr Gleason. He pedalled back and asked him to attend a dance that was to be held on the next Friday, but Mr Gleason said he didn't dance.

"Oh well," my father said, "any time, just drop over."

Mr Gleason went back to supervising his family of Chinese labourers on his wall.

Bald Hill towered high above the town and from my father's small filling station you could sit and watch the wall going up. It was an interesting sight. I watched it for two years, while I waited for customers who rarely came. After school and on Saturdays I had all the time in the world to watch the agonizing progress of Mr Gleason's wall. It was as painful as a clock. Sometimes I could see the Chinese labourers running at a jog-trot carrying bricks on long wooden planks. The hill was bare, and on this bareness Mr Gleason was, for some reason, building a wall.

In the beginning people thought it peculiar that someone would build such a big wall on Bald Hill. The only thing to recommend Bald Hill was the view of the town, and Mr Gleason was building a wall that denied that view. The top soil was thin and bare clay showed through in places. Nothing would ever grow there. Everyone assumed that Gleason had simply gone mad and after the initial interest they accepted his madness as they accepted his wall and as they accepted Bald Hill itself.

Occasionally someone would pull in for petrol at my father's filling station and ask about the wall and my father would shrug and I would see, once more, the strangeness of it.

"A house?" the stranger would ask. "Up on that hill?"

"No," my father would say, "chap named Gleason is building a wall."

And the strangers would want to know why, and my father would shrug and look up at Bald Hill once more. "Damned if I know," he'd say.

Gleason still lived in his old house at Mason's Lane. It was a plain weatherboard house with a rose garden at the front, a vegetable garden down the side, and an orchard at the back.

At night we kids would sometimes ride out to Bald Hill on our bicycles. It was an agonizing, muscle-twitching ride, the worst part of which was a steep, unmade road up which we finally pushed our bikes, our lungs rasping in the night air. When we arrived we found nothing but walls. Once we broke down some of the brickwork and another time we threw stones at the tents where the Chinese labourers slept. Thus we expressed our frustration at this inexplicable thing.

The wall must have been finished on the day before my twelfth birthday. I remember going on a picnic birthday party up to Eleven Mile Creek and we lit a fire and cooked chops at a bend in the river from where it was possible to see the walls on Bald Hill. I remember standing with a hot chop in my hand and someone saying, "Look, they're leaving!"

We stood on the creek bed and watched the Chinese labourers walking their bicycles slowly down the hill. Someone said they were going to build a chimney up at the mine at A.1 and certainly there is a large brick chimney there now, so I suppose they built it.

When the word spread that the walls were finished most of the town went up to look. They walked around the four walls which were as interesting as any other brick walls. They stood in front of the big wooden gates and tried to peer through, but all they could see was a small blind wall that had obviously been constructed for this special purpose. The walls themselves were ten feet high and topped with broken glass and barbed wire. When it became obvious that we were not going to discover the contents of the enclosure, we all gave up and went home.

Mr Gleason had long since stopped coming into town. His wife came instead, wheeling a pram down from Mason's Lane to Main Street and filling it with groceries and meat (they never bought vegetables, they grew their own) and wheeling it back to Mason's Lane. Sometimes you would see her standing with the pram halfway up the Gell Street hill. Just standing there, catching her breath. No one asked her about the wall. They knew she wasn't responsible for the wall and they felt sorry for her, having to bear the burden of the pram and her husband's madness. Even when she began to visit Dixon's hardware and buy plaster of paris and tins of paint and water-proofing compound, no one asked her what these things were for. She had a way of averting her eyes that indicated her terror of questions. Old Dixon carried the plaster of paris and the tins of paint out to her pram for her and watched her push them away. "Poor woman," he said, "poor bloody woman."

From the filling station where I sat dreaming in the sun, or from the enclosed office where I gazed mournfully at the rain, I would see, occasionally, Gleason entering or leaving his walled compound, a tiny figure way up on Bald Hill. And I'd think "Gleason", but not much more.

Occasionally strangers drove up there to see what was going on, often egged on by locals who told them it was a Chinese temple or some other silly thing. Once a group of Italians had a picnic outside the walls and took photographs of each other standing in front of the closed door. God knows what they thought it was.

But for five years between my twelfth and seventeenth birthdays there was nothing to interest me in Gleason's walls. Those years seem lost to me now and I can remember very little of them. I developed a crush on Susy Markin and followed her back from the swimming pool on my bicycle. I sat behind her in the pictures and wandered past her house. Then her parents moved to another town and I sat in the sun and waited for them to come back.

We became very keen on modernization. When coloured paints became available the whole town went berserk and brightly coloured houses blossomed overnight. But the paints were not of good quality and quickly faded and peeled, so that the town looked like a garden of dead flowers. Thinking of those years, the only real thing I recall is the soft hiss of bicycle tyres on the main street. When I think of it now it seems very peaceful, but I remember then that the sound induced in me a feeling of melancholy, a feeling somehow mixed with the early afternoons when the sun went down behind Bald Hill and the town felt as sad as an empty dance hall on a Sunday afternoon.

And then, during my seventeenth year, Mr Gleason died. We found out when we saw Mrs Gleason's pram parked out in front of Phonsey Joy's Funeral Parlour. It looked very sad, that pram, standing by itself in the windswept street. We came and looked at the pram and felt sad for Mrs Gleason. She hadn't had much of a life.

Phonsey Joy carried old Mr Gleason out to the cemetery by the Parwan Railway Station and Mrs Gleason rode behind in a taxi. People watched the old hearse go by and thought, "Gleason", but not much else.

And then, less than a month after Gleason had been buried out at the lonely cemetery by the Parwan Railway Station, the Chinese labourers came back. We saw them push their bicycles up the hill. I stood with my father and Phonsey Joy and wondered what was going on.

And then I saw Mrs Gleason trudging up the hill. I nearly didn't recognize her, because she didn't have her pram. She carried a black umbrella and walked slowly up Bald Hill and it wasn't until she stopped for breath and leant forward that I recognized her.

"It's Mrs Gleason," I said, "with the Chinese."

But it wasn't until the next morning that it became obvious what was happening. People lined the main street in the way they do for a big funeral but, instead of gazing towards the Grant Street corner, they all looked up at Bald Hill.

All that day and all the next people gathered to watch the destruction of the walls. They saw the Chinese labourers darting to and fro, but it wasn't until they knocked down a large section of the wall facing the town that we realized there really was something inside. It was impossible to see what it was, but there was something there. People stood and wondered and pointed out Mrs Gleason to each other as she went to and fro supervising the work.

And finally, in ones and twos, on bicycles and on foot, the whole town moved up to Bald Hill. Mr Dyer closed up his butcher shop and my father got out the old Chev truck and we finally arrived up at Bald Hill with twenty people on board. They crowded into the back tray and hung on to the running boards and my father grimly steered his way through the crowds of bicycles and parked just where the dirt track gets really steep. We trudged up this last steep track, never for a moment suspecting what we would find at the top.

It was very quiet up there. The Chinese labourers worked diligently, removing the third and fourth walls and cleaning the bricks which they stacked neatly in big piles. Mrs Gleason said nothing either. She stood in the only remaining corner of the walls and looked defiantly at the townspeople who stood open-mouthed where another corner had been.

And between us and Mrs Gleason was the most incredibly beautiful thing I had ever seen in my life. For one moment I didn't recognize it. I stood open-mouthed, and breathed the surprising beauty of it. And then I realized it was our town. The buildings were two feet high and they were a little rough but very correct. I saw Mr Dyer nudge my father and whisper that Gleason had got the faded "U" in the BUTCHER sign of his shop.

I think at that moment everyone was overcome with a feeling

of simple joy. I can't remember ever having felt so uplifted and happy. It was perhaps a childish emotion but I looked up at my father and saw a smile of such warmth spread across his face that I knew he felt just as I did. Later he told me that he thought Gleason had built the model of our town just for this moment, to let us see the beauty of our own town, to make us proud of ourselves and to stop the American Dreams we were so prone to. For the rest, my father said, was not Gleason's plan and he could not have foreseen the things that happened afterwards.

I have come to think that this view of my father's is a little sentimental and also, perhaps, insulting to Gleason. I personally believe that he knew everything that would happen. One day the proof of my theory may be discovered. Certainly there are in existence some personal papers, and I firmly believe that these papers will show that Gleason knew exactly what would happen.

We had been so overcome by the model of the town that we hadn't noticed what was the most remarkable thing of all. Not only had Gleason built the houses and the shops of our town, he had also peopled it. As we tip-toed into the town we suddenly found ourselves. "Look," I said to Mr Dyer, "there you are."

And there he was, standing in front of his shop in his apron. As I bent down to examine the tiny figure I was staggered by the look on its face. The modelling was crude, the paintwork was sloppy, and the face a little too white, but the expression was absolutely perfect: those pursed, quizzical lips and the eyebrows lifted high. It was Mr Dyer and no one else on earth.

And there beside Mr Dyer was my father, squatting on the footpath and gazing lovingly at Mr Dyer's bicycle's gears, his face marked with grease and hope.

And there was I, back at the filling station, leaning against a petrol pump in an American pose and talking to Brian Sparrow who was amusing me with his clownish antics.

Phonsey Joy standing beside his hearse. Mr Dixon sitting inside his hardware store. Everyone I knew was there in that tiny town. If they were not in the streets or in their backyards they were inside their houses, and it didn't take very long to discover that you could lift off the roofs and peer inside.

We tip-toed around the streets peeping into each other's windows, lifting off each other's roofs, admiring each other's gardens, and, while we did it, Mrs Gleason slipped silently away down the hill towards Mason's Lane. She spoke to nobody and nobody spoke to her.

I confess that I was the one who took the roof from Cavanagh's house. So I was the one who found Mrs Cavanagh in bed with young Craigie Evans.

I stood there for a long time, hardly knowing what I was seeing. I stared at the pair of them for a long, long time. And when I finally knew what I was seeing I felt such an incredible mixture of jealousy and guilt and wonder that I didn't know what to do with the roof.

Eventually it was Phonsey Joy who took the roof from my hands and placed it carefully back on the house, much, I imagine, as he would have placed the lid on a coffin. By then other people had seen what I had seen and the word passed around very quickly.

And then we all stood around in little groups and regarded the model town with what could only have been fear. If Gleason knew about Mrs Cavanagh and Craigie Evans (and no one else had), what other things might he know? Those who hadn't seen themselves yet in the town began to look a little nervous and were unsure of whether to look for themselves or not. We gazed silently at the roofs and felt mistrustful and guilty.

We all walked down the hill then, very quietly, the way people walk away from a funeral, listening only to the crunch of the gravel under our feet while the women had trouble with their high-heeled shoes.

The next day a special meeting of the shire council passed a motion calling on Mrs Gleason to destroy the model town on the grounds that it contravened building regulations.

It is unfortunate that this order wasn't carried out before the city newspapers found out. Before another day had gone by the government had stepped in.

The model town and its model occupants were to be preserved. The minister for tourism came in a large black car and made a speech to us in the football pavilion. We sat on the high, tiered seats eating potato chips while he stood against the fence and talked to us. We couldn't hear him very well, but we heard enough. He called the model town a work of art and we stared at him grimly. He said it would be an invaluable tourist attraction. He said tourists would come from everywhere to see the model town. We would be famous. Our businesses would flourish. There would be work for guides and interpreters and caretakers and taxi drivers and people selling soft drinks and ice creams.

The Americans would come, he said. They would visit our town in buses and in cars and on the train. They would take photographs and bring wallets bulging with dollars. American dollars.

We looked at the minister mistrustfully, wondering if he knew about Mrs Cavanagh, and he must have seen the look because he said that certain controversial items would be removed, had already been removed. We shifted in our seats, like you do when a particularly tense part of a film has come to its climax, and then we relaxed and listened to what the minister had to say. And we all began, once more, to dream our American Dreams.

We saw our big smooth cars cruising through cities with bright lights. We entered expensive night clubs and danced till dawn. We made love to women like Kim Novak and men like Rock Hudson. We drank cocktails. We gazed lazily into refrigerators filled with food and prepared ourselves lavish midnight snacks which we ate while we watched huge television sets on which we would be able to see American movies free of charge and forever.

The minister, like someone from our American Dreams, re-entered his large black car and cruised slowly from our humble sportsground, and the newspaper men arrived and swarmed over the pavilion with their cameras and notebooks. They took photographs of us and photographs of the models up on Bald Hill. And the next day we were all over the newpapers. The photogaphs of the model people side by side with photographs of the real people. And our names and ages and what we did were all printed there in black and white.

They interviewed Mrs Gleason but she said nothing of interest. She said the model town had been her husband's hobby.

We all felt good now. It was very pleasant to have your photograph in the paper. And, once more, we changed our opinion of Gleason. The shire council held another meeting and named the dirt track up Bald Hill, "Gleason Avenue". Then we all went home and waited for the Americans we had been promised.

It didn't take long for them to come, although at the time it seemed an eternity, and we spent six long months doing nothing more with our lives than waiting for the Americans.

Well, they did come. And let me tell you how it has all worked out for us.

The Americans arrive every day in buses and cars and sometimes the younger ones come on the train. There is now a small airstrip out near the Parwan cemetery and they also arrive there, in small aeroplanes. Phonsey Joy drives them to the cemetery where they look at Gleason's grave and then up to Bald Hill and then down to the town. He is doing very well from it all. It is good to see someone doing well from it. Phonsey is becoming a big man in town and is on the shire council.

On Bald Hill there are half a dozen telescopes through which the Americans can spy on the town and reassure themselves that it is the same down there as it is on Bald Hill. Herb Gravney sells them ice creams and soft drinks and extra film for their cameras. He is another one who is doing well. He bought the whole model from Mrs Gleason and charges five American dollars admission. Herb is on the council now too. He's doing very well for himself. He sells them the film so they can take photographs of the houses and the model people and so they can come down to the town with their special maps and hunt out the real people.

To tell the truth most of us are pretty sick of the game. They come looking for my father and ask him to stare at the gears of Dyer's bicycle. I watch my father cross the street slowly, his head hung low. He doesn't greet the Americans any more. He doesn't ask them questions about colour television or Washington D.C. He kneels on the footpath in front of Dyer's bike. They stand around him. Often they remember the model incorrectly and try to get my father to pose in the wrong way. Originally he argued with them, but now he argues no more. He does what they ask. They push him this way and that and worry about the expression on his face which is no longer what it was.

Then I know they will come to find me. I am next on the map. I am very popular for some reason. They come in search of me and my petrol pump as they have done for four years now. I do not await them eagerly because I know, before they reach me, that they will be disappointed.

"But this is not the boy."

"Yes," says Phonsey, "this is him alright." And he gets me to show them my certificate.

They examine the certificate suspiciously, feeling the paper as if it might be a clever forgery. "No," they declare. (Americans are so confident.) "No," they shake their heads, "this is not the real boy. The real boy is younger."

"He's older now. He used to be younger." Phonsey looks weary when he tells them. He can afford to look weary.

The Americans peer at my face closely. "It's a different boy."

But finally they get their cameras out. I stand sullenly and try to look amused as I did once. Gleason saw me looking amused but I can no longer remember how it felt. I was looking at Brian Sparrow. But Brian is also tired. He finds it difficult to do his clownish antics and to the Americans his little act isn't funny. They prefer the model. I watch him sadly, sorry that he must perform for such an unsympathetic audience.

The Americans pay one dollar for the right to take our photographs. Having paid the money they are worried about being cheated. They spend their time being disappointed and I spend my time feeling guilty that I have somehow let them down by growing older and sadder.

War Crimes

1

In the end I shall be judged.

They will write about me in books and take care to explain me so badly that it is better that I do it myself. They will write with the stupid smugness of middle-class intellectuals, people of moral rectitude who have never seriously placed themselves at risk. They have supported wars they have not fought in, and damned companies they have not had the courage to destroy. Their skins are fair and pampered and their bellies are corseted by expensively made jeans.

They will write about me as a tyrant, a psychopath, an aberrant accountant, and many other things, but it would never once occur to them that I might know exactly what I am doing. Neither would they imagine that I might have feelings other than those of a mad dog.

But they do not have a monopoly on finer feelings, as you shall soon see.

I cannot begin to tell you how I loathe them, how I have, in weaker moments, envied them, how I longed to be accepted by them and how at the first hint of serious threat from them I would not have the faintest qualms about incarcerating them all.

The vermin, may they feast on this and cover it with their idiot footnotes.

2

The most elegant Barto was driving the car, a Cadillac Eldorado with leaking air-conditioning. In a purple T-shirt and waist-length fur coat, he looked the very embodiment of sexual decadence; his shoulder-length raven hair, his large nose and chin made him as severely handsome as an Indian on a postage stamp.

Beside him, I felt graceless and boring. My jeans, no less old than his, were shapeless and baggy. My hair was tangled and knotted, my glasses filthy, and my unshaven face looked pasty, patchy and particularly unhealthy. It was a face made to appear in the dock, a poor man's face, squinting nervously into the future.

I had filled the trunk of the Eldorado with an armory of modern weapons but I carried a small ·22 under my arm. The ·22 is a punk's weapon. It was my secret and I shared it with no one.

Barto kept a Colt ·45 in the glove box. It was big and heavy and perfectly melodramatic. "If it doesn't scare the cunts to death we can always shoot them."

It was a hard time and only the most unconventional methods were succeeding in business. Certainly we didn't look like the popular image of businessmen. We were special. Once you appreciated the power we held, you could only be astonished at our cleverness. For me, my grubbiness had become a habit so long ingrained that it is difficult to think back to how it started or why it continued. But it was, finally, a perverse identification with the poor people I was raised amongst. Excepting the years when I was a young accountant, I have continued to wear the marks of my caste for they are stamped, not only on my face, but also on my poorly-fed bones. No matter what rich clothes I wore, I would deceive no one. So I wear them proudly. They stink. The most casual observer will know that I am someone of great note: to dress like a beggar and be given the accord due to a prince. It was a costume fit for an age which had begun by proudly proclaiming its lack of regimentation and ended railing at its own disarray.

They were, surely, the Last Days.

Unemployment had become a way of life and the vagabonds had formed into bands with leaders, organizations and even, in some cases, apocalyptic religions whose leaders preached the coming of the millennium. These last were as rare as threatened species, cosseted, protected and filmed by bored journalists eager for symbols of the times. The rest of the bands roamed the country, godless, hungry and unpublicized.

We saw only one group on the six-hundred-mile journey north. They were camped by a bridge at the Thirty-Two Mile Creek. As we approached they attempted to drag a dead tree across the road.

I felt Bart hesitate. The cowboy boot came back off the accelerator, making a stoned decision at sixty miles an hour.

"Plant it," I said. I said it fast and hard.

He planted it. The Cadillac responded perfectly. I heard the crunch of breaking wood. Tearing noises. Looking back I saw two bundles of rags lying on the road.

"Shit." The word was very quiet. I looked at Bart. He looked a little pale.

"How did it feel?"

He considered my question. "I don't know," he drawled out the words, beginning to luxuriate in the puzzle they contained, "just sort of *soft*. Sort of . . ." he furrowed his brow, "sort of did-it-happen, didn't-it-happen type of thing."

I leant into the back seat and pulled up a bag of dope and rolled an exceedingly large trumpet-shaped joint. The Cadillac devoured the miles while the faulty air-conditioner dripped cold water on to Bart's cowboy boots, and I thought once again how genuinely strange our lives had become. I often stepped back and looked at myself from the outside. I was unthinkable to myself. Now I found it amazing to consider that only a week ago I had been making a most unconventional presentation to a highly conservative board of directors. The success of the presentation was the reason we were now heading north in this elegant motor car.

The board, of course, knew a great deal about us before we made the presentation. They were prepared for, and wanted, the unconventional. They expected to be frightened. They also expected to be given hope. Given their desire to believe in us, it would have been exceedingly difficult to do the presentation badly.

I dressed as badly as they would have expected me to, and spoke as arrogantly as they had been led to expect I would. There was nothing terribly original in the way we analysed the ills of the frozen-meals subsidiary. It was simply professional, a quality that was lacking in the subsidiary's present management. We presented a market analysis, and pointed out that their company was in a unique position to take advantage of the present economic conditions. We presented a profit projection for the next twelve months and claimed a fee of half this figure, or of whatever profit was finally delivered. If there was no profit we would ask for no fee. This money was to be delivered to us, in whatever way their lawyers could discover, tax free.

We demanded complete autonomy during those twelve months and asked the board's guarantee that they would not interfere.

It was not difficult to imagine that they would buy it. They were making heavy losses and we were obviously confident of making considerable profits. In addition I had two successes behind me: a pharmaceutical company and a supermarket chain, both of which had been rescued from the hands of the receivers and turned into profitable businesses.

It would never have occurred to them that now, on this road heading towards their factory, I would be so tense and nervous that my stomach would hurt. I had gained a perverse pleasure from their respect. Now I would live in terror of losing it.

Outside the car, the scrub was immersed in a hot haze. The world seemed full of poisonous spiders, venomous snakes, raw red clay, and the bitter desperate faces of disenfranchised men.

3

The factory belched smoke into the sky and looked beyond saving. We parked by the bridge and watched white-coated men in an aluminium boat inspect the dead fish which were floating there.

The dead fish and the foul smoke from the plant assumed the nature of a feverish dream. Flies descended on our shirt backs and our faces. We waved at them distractedly. Through the heat-haze I observed the guard at the factory gate. His scuttling behaviour seemed as alien and inexplicable as that of a tropical crab. It took some time to realize that we were the object of his uncertain attentions: he kept walking out towards us and shouting. When we didn't respond, he quickly lost all courage and nervously scuttled back to his post.

The Cadillac was confusing him.

Around the plant the country was scrubby, dense, prickly and unattractive. Certain grasses betrayed the presence of swamp and the air itself was excessively humid and almost clinging. The prospect of spending twelve months here was not a pleasant one.

Behind the anxious guard the factory stood quietly rusting under a heavy grey sky. It looked like nothing more than a collection of eccentric tin huts. One might expect them to contain something dusty and rotten, the left-overs from a foreign war in disordered heaps, broken instruments with numbered dials and stiff canvas webbing left to slowly rust and decay.

Yet the plant was the largest frozen-food processing and storage facility in the country. The storerooms, at this moment, contained one and a half million dollars worth of undistributed merchandise, household favourites that had lost their popularity in the market place. It was hard to reconcile the appearance of the plant with the neat spiral-bound report titled "Production and Storage Facilities".

I knew at that moment I didn't want to go anywhere near that plant. I wanted to be in a nice bar with soft music playing, the air-conditioning humming, a little bowl of macadamia nuts and a very long gin and tonic in front of me. I got back into the Cadillac and took some Mylanta for my stomach.

At the gate the guard seemed reluctant to let us in and Bart pulled out the Colt. It was an unnecessary move but he enjoyed it. His gangster fantasies had never been allowed for in corporate life.

He looked like a prince of darkness, standing at the gate in a purple T-shirt, a fur coat, the fingernails of his gun hand painted in green and blue. I smiled watching him, thinking that capitalism had surely entered its most picturesque phase.

4

The hate in the staff canteen was as palpable as the humidity outside. It buzzed and stung, finding weak spots in my carefully prepared defences. We had played the videotape with the chairman's speech to the employees but it did nothing to dilute the feelings of the office staff who behaved like a subject race.

The girls giggled rudely. The men glowered, pretending to misunderstand the nature of the orders we gave them. I felt that their threat might, at any instant, become physical and an attack be made. Barto, more agitated than usual, produced the ·45. He was laughed at. He stood there aghast, no longer feeling as cool as he would have liked.

It was a particularly bad start. I requested the sales, marketing and production managers to escort me to my new office where we could discuss their futures.

When I left the canteen I was burning with a quiet rage. My hands were wet. My stomach hurt. I was more than a little frightened. I began to understand why men raze villages and annihilate whole populations. The ·22 under my arm nagged at me, producing feelings that were intense, unnameable, and not totally unpleasurable.

5

I fed on my fear and used it to effect. It was my strength. It hardened me and kept my mind sharp and clear. It gave me the confidence of cornered men. It made sleep almost impossible.

We worked from the old general manager's office, the brown smudge of his suicide an unpleasant reminder of the possibility of failure. We found the floor more convenient than the desk and spread papers across it as we attempted to piece the mess together.

It became obvious very early that the marketing manager was a fool. His understanding of conditions in the market place was minimal. His foolishly optimistic report had been a major contributing factor in the present state of affairs.

He had taken too many store buyers to too many lunches. It must have been a little awkward for the buyers to tell him they weren't taking any more of his products.

It was also difficult for me to tell him that he could not continue as marketing manager. He was large and weak and watery. He had the softness of those who lie long hours in hot baths before dressing carefully in tailormade suits. He could not adjust to me. He could not think of me as a threat, merely as someone who needed a wash. When I dismissed him he did not understand.

He returned to his office the next day and continued as usual.

When you kill flathead you put a knife in their foreheads. Their eyes roll and sometimes pop out. The marketing manager reacted in a similar manner when it occurred to him that he was being fired. His mouth opened wide with shock and I was reminded of a flathead when I looked at his eyes.

As with the fish, I found it necessary not to think too much about what I was doing. I consoled myself with the knowledge that there would have been no job for him if we had not arrived. He had been thorough enough to have destroyed any hope of his own survival. He had covered it from every angle.

With the marketing manager's departure I discovered a whole filing cabinet full of documents that he had withheld from me. As I examined them I felt like a surgeon who comes to remove a small growth and finds a body riddled with secondary cancers. I had promised the board of directors things which, given all the available information, had seemed reasonable at the time. But here the gap between the diseased body and my promises of glowing health seemed an inseparable gulf.

I began to feel that I might be less remarkable than the glorious picture the board had of me. When I had presented my credentials and broad methods to them I had felt myself to be quite glamorous, a superior being who could succeed where they and their underlings had failed. It was a good picture. I preened myself before it as if it were a mirror.

I claimed to despise the board but I didn't want that mirror taken away from me. It was very important that they hold me in high esteem.

Incensed by the appalling news we found in marketing, we recalled the sales force and threatened them with violence and torture if they did not succeed. I am thin and not particularly strong but I had a gun and I had the genuine craziness of a man who will do anything to get what he wants. Anger filled me like electricity. My fingertips were full of it. They felt so tight and tense I couldn't keep them still. Bart stood smoking a joint and waving the Colt around the office with the most carefree abandon, sighting down the barrel at first one head and then another. We spoke to them quietly and politely about the sales targets we expected them to meet in the coming year.

Whether through accident or design. Bart let off a shot into the ceiling and the sales manager involuntarily wet his pants. His staff laughed out loud at his misfortune. I thought how ugly they looked with their big cufflinks and silly grins.

It was not the ideal way to do business, but the times were hard, other job opportunities non-existent, and the competition in the trade intense. Our products had been de-listed by five major chains and were in danger of being kicked out of another three. Only our cheapest lines survived, and these—frozen dinners of exceptionally low quality and price—would have to spearhead our return to the market. They were cheap and filling and there were a lot of people who needed cheap filling meals.

I gave Bart control of the marketing function and watched him nervously like a driver who takes his hands from the wheel but is ready to take it back at any serious deviation. Apart from twelve months as a trainee product manager with Procter and Gamble, Bart's previous experience had been totally in advertising agencies. There was really nothing but my intuitive judgement to say that he'd be a success in this new role.

I needn't have worried. He had a business brain the like of which is rarely seen, as cool and clean as stainless steel and totally without compassion. It was Bart who dumped two warehouses full of frozen food straight into the river, thus clearing a serious bottleneck in the system and creating space for products that could actually be sold. He budgeted for the $200 fine and spent another $200 on the finest cocaine to celebrate with. I approved these expenses without question. The goods had been sitting in the warehouse for two years and had been written down in value by a thoughtful accountant who seemed the only person to have anticipated the company's present plight.

Bart doubled the advertising budget, a move which terrified me but which I approved. He planned to drop advertising altogether in the second half and plough an equivalent amount into promotions. It was pressure-cooked marketing. It was unorthodox and expensive but it was the sort of brutal tactic that could be necessary for our success.

Bart pursued the practice of business with the logic of an abstract artist. Things were, for him, problems of form, colour and design. He pursued cool acts with relentless enthusiasm.

From my office I watched him walk across the wide bitumen apron to fire the production manager. His hair was now dyed a henna red, and his cowboy boots made his out-turned toes look curiously elegant. He walked as casually as a man who has run out of cigarette papers taking a stroll to a corner shop.

6

The typists had stopped staring at us and were actually managing to get some work done. However I still continued to have trouble with my secretary. She was nearly forty-five, matronly in style, and as the secretary to the most senior executive, she was the leader of the others. She was pursuing some guerrilla war of her own, expressing her distaste for me in a hundred little ways which were almost impossible to confront directly.

On this occasion she found me alone in my office. I was sitting on the floor going through the computer print-outs from the Nielsen survey when she crept up behind me and hissed in my ear.

"May I have a word."

The bitch. She made me jump. I turned in time to catch the last sign of a smirk disappearing from her face.

I stood up. The idea of looking up her dress was beyond contemplation. I thought, as I stumbled to my feet, that I should fire her or at least exchange her with someone who could handle her. As she continued to disapprove of me she was making me more and more irritable. Yet she seemed able to bully me. I felt awkward and embarrassed every time I talked to her.

"I think," she declared, "there is something you should know."

"Yes." I put the Nielsen survey carefully on the desk. Her face was pinched and her lips had become tightly pursed. If there had been a smirk it had well and truly been superseded by this angry, self-righteous expression.

"I have come to tell you that I can't work for you." I felt enormously relieved. "I'm sorry to hear that," I said.

"I don't suppose you'd be interested in why."

"Yes, of course I would."

This would be her moment and I would pay attention. I did as she wished.

"I cannot respect you." Her sanctimonious little face gave me the shits.

"Oh," I said, "and why not?"

"Because you are not worthy of respect." She stood stiffly upright, tapping her lolly pink suit with a ballpoint pen which was putting little blue flecks all over it.

"You don't respect yourself." She cast a derisive glance over me as if I were someone at the back door begging for sandwiches. So she didn't like the way I dressed. "You don't respect yourself, how can I respect you."

"Oh," I laughed, "I respect myself, please don't concern yourself on that one."

"You've obviously had a good education. Why don't you use it?"

She was beginning to push it a bit far. Her complete ridiculousness didn't stop her from upsetting me. I should have been beyond all this. "I'm your general manager," I said, "surely that's using my education."

She tossed her head. "Ah, but you're not the *real* general manager."

She shouldn't have upset me at all. Her values were nothing like mine. She was trapped and helpless and had to work for me. She had no education, no chance of change. All she had was the conviction that I was worthless. It shouldn't have upset me, but it is exactly the sort of thing that upsets me. The thing she wouldn't give me was the only thing I wanted from her. I felt my temper welling up.

"Do you realize the power I have over you?" I asked her.

"You have no power over me, young man."

She didn't understand me. She thought I was just a scruffy hippy who had come to make a mess in her old boss's office. She couldn't know that I have a terrible character weakness, a temper that comes from nowhere and stuns even me with its ferocity and total unreasonableness.

She shouldn't have spoken to me like that, but she wouldn't stop. She wouldn't leave when I asked her to. I stood in my office and I asked the old bitch to leave. I asked her cooly and nicely and politely, but she continued to berate me.

I watched her mouth move. It became unreal. I had the ·22 under my arm, and my feelings were not like the real world, they were hot and pleasurable and electrically intense.

It was rage.

She had just repeated herself. She had just said something about respect when I drew the pistol and shot her in the foot.

She stopped talking. I watched the red mark on her stockinged foot and thought how amazingly accurate I had been.

She sat on the floor with surprise and a slight grunt.

Barto came running through the door and I stood there with the gun in my hand feeling stupid.

Later the incident made me think about myself and what I wanted from life.

7

The provincial city nearest the plant was a most unappealing place, catering to the tastes of farmers and factory hands. We devised, therefore, quarters of our own at the plant itself and managed to create a very pleasant island within the administration block.

Here a quite unique little society began to evolve, hidden from a hostile environment by dull red-brick walls. Here we devoted ourselves to the pursuit of good talk, fanciful ideas and the appreciation of good music.

We introduced fine old Baluchi rugs, rich in colour, others from Shiraz, Luristan, old Kilims, mellow and pleasant, glowing like jewels. Here we had huge couches and leather armchairs, soft and old and vibrating with the dying snores of retired soldiers, the suppleness of ancient leathers a delight to the senses. We had low, slow, yellow lights, as gentle as moonlight, and stereo equipment, its fidelity best evoked by considering the sound of Tibetan temple bells. The food, at first, was largely indifferent but the drugs and wine were always plentiful, of extraordinary variety and excellent quality.

In these conditions we marvelled at ourselves, that we, the sons of process workers and hotel-keepers, should live like this.

We were still young enough to be so entranced by our success and Barto, whose father sold stolen goods in a series of hotels, was eager that a photograph be taken.

Barto seemed the most innocent of men. He approached life languidly, rarely rising before ten and never retiring before three. Ideas came from him in vast numbers and hardly ever appeared to be anything but wisps of smoke.

Lying on the great Baluchi saddle-bag, graceful as a cat in repose, he would begin by saying, "What if . . ." It was normally Bart who said "What if . . ." and normally me who said "Yes" or "no". His mind was relentless in its logic, yet fanciful in style, so the most circuitous and fanciful plans would always, on examination, be found to have cold hard bones within their diaphanous folds.

We were all-powerful. We only had to dream and the dream could be made real. We planned the most unlikely strategies and carried them out, whole plots as involved and chancy as movie scenarios. It was our most remarkable talent. For instance, we evolved a plan for keeping a defecting product manager faithful by getting him a three-bag smack habit and then supplying it.

Our character judgement was perfect. We were delighted by our astuteness.

The product manager stayed but unfortunately killed himself a few months later, so not everything worked out as perfectly as we would have hoped.

We saw ourselves anew, mirrored in the eyes of each new arrival and we preened ourselves before their gaze.

Thelma was the first to arrive. She came to be with Bart and was astounded, firstly by the ugliness of the plant, secondly by the beauty of our private world, and thirdly by the change she claimed had occurred in Bart. She found him obsessed with the business enterprise and unbearably arrogant about his part in it. This she blamed me for. She sat in a corner whispering with Bart and I fretted lest she persuade him to go away with her. She was slender and elegant and dark as a gypsy. She had little needle tracks on her arms, so later on I was able to do a deal with her whereby she agreed to go away for a while.

Ian arrived to take over the sales force and we delighted in his company. He thought our methods of enthusing the salesmen historically necessary but not the most productive in the long term. He took them fifteen miles into town and got drunk with them for two days. He had two fist fights and, somewhere along the line, lost the representative for southern country districts, a point he continued to remain vague about.

He was the perfect chameleon and won them over by becoming vulgar and loud-mouthed. He affected big cufflinks and changed his shirt twice a day. He had his hair cut perfectly and he looked handsome and macho with his smiling dark eyes.

The sales force loved him, having the mistaken idea that he was normal. Naturally he didn't discuss his enthusiastic appetite for a substance called ACP, a veterinary tranquillizer normally administered to nervous horses which he took, rather ostentatiously, from a teaspoon marked "Souvenir of Anglesea".

It was Ian who persuaded me to fly in Sergei from Hong Kong. With his arrival, a huge weight was lifted from my shoulders and I had more time to relax and enjoy the music and talk. Sergei was unknown to me and I found him, in some respects, alarming. It was as if he found nothing remarkable in our situation. He made no comment on the decor of our private quarters, our penchant for drugs, or the brilliance of our strategies. It was as if we stood before a mirror which reflected everything but ourselves. He made me nervous. I didn't know how I stood with him.

Yet he was the most ordinary of men: short, slim, and dark, moving with a preciseness which I found comforting in such a skilled accountant. He was eccentric in his dress, choosing neatly pressed grey flannel trousers, very expensive knitted shirts, and slip-on shoes of the softest leather. Only the small silver earring on his left earlobe gave an indication that he was not totally straight.

Sergei talked little but went quietly about the business of wrestling with our cash flow. In the first week he completely reprogrammed our computer to give us a simpler and faster idea of our situation. Each week's figures would be available on the Monday of the next week, which made life easier for all of us.

After three weeks I gave over the financial function almost completely to his care and tried to spend some time evolving a sensible long term strategy suited to the economic climate we were now likely to live in for some time. It is a curious fact that large companies are very slow to react to changes in the market place.

Whilst the unemployed continued to receive government assistance there would be a multimillion dollar business in satisfying their needs. Companies which should have had the sense to see this continued to ignore it. Obviously they viewed the present circumstances as some temporary aberration and were planning their long term strategies in the belief that we would shortly be returning to normal market conditions.

My view was that we were experiencing "normal" market conditions.

I instructed our new product development team to investigate the possibility of producing a range of very simple frozen meals which would be extremely filling, could be eaten cold when cooking facilities were not available, and would be lower in cost than anything comparable. I had a series of pie-like dishes in mind but I left the brief open. It seemed like a golden opportunity.

While I was engaged in this, word came from Ian that they had had a highly successful sell-in of our existing lines of frozen meals. He had given the trade substantial discounts and we were operating on very low profit margins, hoping to achieve a very high volume turnover, and more importantly get our relationship with the trade back to a healthier state.

The telex from Ian was very short: "They love us till their balls ache. Sell-in is 180 per cent of forecast."

I looked out my window as Barto and Sergei walked towards the storeroom which hid the plant itself from my view. Bart's Colt now sat snugly in a hand-tooled leather holster he had spent the last few nights making.

Beside Bart's pointy-toed languid walk, Sergei looked as strict as a wound-up toy.

I watched them thoughtfully, thinking that they had the comic appearance of truly lethal things.

8

My father lost his hand in a factory. He carried the stump with him as a badge of his oppression by factories. When I was very small I saw that my father had no hand and concluded that my hand would also be cut off when the time came. I carried this belief quietly in the dark part of my mind reserved for dreadful truths. Thus it was with a most peculiar and personal interest that I watched the beheading of chickens, the amputation of fox-terriers' tails, and even the tarring of young lambs. My fear was so intense that all communication on the subject was unthinkable. It would be done just as they had mutilated my cock by cutting off the skin on its head.

I envied my two sisters, who, I was sure, would be allowed to have two hands like my mother.

The factories my father worked in were many and various. I remember only their dark cavernous doors, their dull, hot, metal exteriors, the various stinks they left in my father's hair, and the tired sour smell of sweaty clothes that could never be washed often enough.

In the sleep-out behind the house I pinned pictures of motor cars to the walls and masturbated. The yellow walls were decorated with dull brown ageing Sellotape and the breasts of impossible girls even less attainable than the motor cars. It was here that I waited to be sent to the factory. Here on hot, stinking afternoons I planned the most fantastic escapes and the most blood-curdling retaliations. It was here, at night, that I was struck dumb by nightmares. The nightmares that assailed me were full of factories which, never really seen and only imagined, were more horrifying than anything my father could have encountered. They cut and slashed at me with gleaming blades and their abysses and chasms gaped before my fearful feet. Their innards were vast and measureless, and they contained nothing but the machinery of mutilation.

The dreams pursued me throughout life and now, at thirty, I still have the same horrible nameless nightmare I first learned when I was five years old. I play it as if it were the music of hell, neatly notated, perfectly repeatable, and as horribly frightening as it was the first time. I am a rabbit caught in the headlights of my dream.

The time had now come to go and confront the factory which was mine. I had done everything in my power to stay away. It was easy enough to make decisions based on engineers' reports and the advice of the production manager. But finally the day came when the excuses began to look ridiculous.

When we left the central admin block the heat came out of the scrubland and hung on us. I had not been outside for three weeks and the heat which I had seen as air-conditioned sunshine now became a very raw reality. A northerly wind lifted stinging dust out of the scrub and flies tried to crawl up my nose and into my ears, as if they wished to lay eggs inside my brain.

The plant and storeroom blinded me with their metallic glare which was not diminished by the streaks of rust decorating their surfaces, hints of some internal disorder.

Barto, walking beside me on the soft, sticky bitumen, said: "How's your nightmare?"

His hair seemed surreal, haloed, blue sky above it and shining silver behind. Already I could hear the rumbling of the plant. A rivulet of dirty water came running from the No. 2 to meet us. Barto hopped across it nimbly, his cowboy boots still immaculately clean.

"Not good," I said. I regretted my confession most bitterly. A confession is nothing but a fart. I have despised those who make confessions of their fears and weaknesses. It is a game the middle class play but they are only manufacturing razor-blades which will be used to slash their own stupid white throats.

The door of the No. 2 yawned cavernous in front of me. The floor was an inch deep in filthy water.

Bart stopped. "Fuck, I can't go in there."

"Why not?" The bastard had to go with me. I wasn't going by myself. We stopped at the door. A foul smell of something cooking came out and engulfed us. I thought I was going to be sick. "Why not?" I asked. "What's the matter?" I tried to make my voice sound normal.

"I'll get my fucking boots fucked." Bart stood at the door, legs apart, a hand on his hip, a knee-cocked, looking down at his cowboy boots. "Fuck," he said, "I'm sorry."

"I'll buy you a new pair." I shouldn't have said that.

"No, there's none left to buy. Shit, I'm sorry." I could see that he was. I could see that there was no way I could talk him into coming with me. I was going to have to do the factory tour alone.

"Fuck your fucking boots."

"I'm sorry. It's just that you can't buy them anymore."

I walked gingerly into the lake and kept going, leaving Bart to feel whatever guilt he was capable of.

In waking life it was not only the machinery I was frightened of, although it was terrifying enough. The vats were huge and their sheer bulk was so unrelated to anything human and I felt my throat block off at the consideration of the weight of food they would contain. The production line itself was also particularly old, clanking, wheezing, full of machinery that oozed grease and farted air, and which lifted and pulled and lifted without any regard for life and limb.

It was the people I didn't want to see.

The heat was impossible, far worse than outside. It mixed with the noise to produce an almost palpable substance which should have suffocated all life. The belt stretched on through this giant corrugated iron oven, and men and women in grubby white stood beside the line, doing operations that had been perfectly described on the production report.

Line No. 3: four female packers, one male supervisor.

The information on the report was enough. It didn't help me to know that one of the female packers was tall and thin with a baleful glare she directed accusingly at management, that her companion was just as tall but heavier, that next to her was a girl of sixteen with wire spectacles and a heat rash that extended from her forehead to her hands, that one other, an olive-skinned girl with a smooth Mediterranean madonna face, would have the foolishness to smile at me. And so on.

I have seen enough factories, god knows, but they continue to be a problem to me. They should not be. My fear is irrational and should be overcome by habituation. But nothing dulls me to the assault of factories and I carry with me, still, the conviction that I will end up at the bottom of the pile, powerless against the machines in factories. So I look at the people a little hard, too searchingly, wondering about them in a way that could make my job impossible. The fish in my hand cannot be thought of as anything more than an operation to be performed. The minute one considers the feelings of the fish the act becomes more difficult. So, in factories, I have a weakness, a hysterical tendency to become the people I see there, to enter their bodies and feel their feelings, and see the never-ending loud, metallic, boring days. And I become bitterly angry for them. And their anger, of course, is directed at me, who isn't them. It is a weakness. A folly. An idiot's hobby.

I got my arse out of the factory as fast as I could.

Bart met me at the door of the No. 2. "How's your nightmare?"

I was still in its grips. I was shaking and angry. "It's really shitty in there. It is *really* shitty."

Bart polished his cowboy boots, rubbing the right toe on the back of his left leg. "What are you going to do about it?" he asked, innocently enough.

A confession is a fart. You should never make a confession, no matter what dope you're on. "I'm not going to do anything, pig face. There's not a fucking thing to do, if I wanted to. That's what factories are like." My suede boots were soaked in muck. I flicked a pea off and watched it bounce across the bitumen.

"Listen," the word drawled out of Bart as slow and lazy as the kicking pointy-toed walk he was walking. The word was inquisitive, tentative, curious and also politely helpful. "Listen, do you think they hate you?"

"Yes." I said it. It slipped out before I had time to think.

"Well," the word came out as lazily as the "listen", "I'll tell you what I'll do in the next two months."

I grinned at him. "What'll you do, smart-arse?"

"I'll fucking make them love you, smart-arse, if that's what you want."

He was grinning delightedly, his hands in his back pockets, his great Indian face turned up towards the screaming sun as if he was drinking power from it.

"And how will you do that?"

"Delegate, delegate," he drawled, "you've got to learn to delegate. Just leave it to me and I'll fix it for you." He finished the conversation in my office. "Easy," he said, "easy-peasy."

9

Almost without noticing it, we became quite famous. This gave me a lot of pleasure, but also disappointed me. You imagine it will amount to more, that it will feel more substantial than it is. This, after all, is the bit you've dreamed of in all the grubby corners of your life. It is almost the reason you've done what you've done. This is where the world is forced to accept you no matter what you wear, no matter what you look like, no matter what your accent is. You re-define what is acceptable. This is when they ask you for your comments on the economy and war and peace, and beautiful girls want to fuck you because you are emanating power which has been the secret of all those strong physiques which you lack, which you needlessly envied. This is what you dreamed about jerking off in your stinking hot bungalow, treasuring your two hands. It is what you told the red-mouthed naked girl in the *Playboy* pin-up when you came all over the glossy page, and what you wished while you wiped the come off the printed image, so as to keep it in good condition for next time.

The middle-class intellectuals were the first to discover us and we were happy enough to have them around. They came up from the south pretending they weren't middle-class. They drank our wine and smoked our dope and drove around in our Cadillac and did tours of the factory. They were most surprised to find that we dressed just like they did. We were flattered that they found us so fascinating and delighted when they were scandalized. In truth we despised them. They were comfortable and had fat-arsed ideas. They went to bed early to read books about people they would try to copy. They didn't bother whether to love or to hate us.

We bought a French chef and we had long dinners with bottles of Château Latour, Corton, Chambertin, and old luscious vintages of Château d'Yquem. They couldn't get over the wine. They raved about it and we played them Dylan.

"Oh Mamma, can this really be the end.
to be stuck inside of Mobile with the Memphis blues again."

We discussed Dada, ecology, Virginia Woolf, Jean-Paul Sartre, Buckminster Fuller, the pan-sexual revolution, Regis Debray, and the whole principle of making stacks of money and going to live in Penang or the south of France.

Occasionally we had rows on important issues and we normally resolved these by the use of violence.

The simplicity of this ploy struck me as obvious and delightful, yet they were too stupid to learn the lessons we could have taught them. They couldn't get past the style. They'd seen too many movies and hung around with too many wardrobe mistresses. They couldn't see or understand that we were no different from Henry Ford or any of the other punks.

They had come to believe that jeans and dope and hair were a sign of some particular integrity. It was a sign of their caste. It confused them.

We were true artists. We showed them the bones of business and power. We instructed them in the use of violence. Metaphorically, we shat with the door open.

They learned nothing, but were attracted to the power with the dumb misunderstanding of lost moths. They criticized us and asked us for jobs.

Finally, of course, the media arrived and allowed themselves to be publicly scandalized by the contradiction in our lives.

The *Late Night* man couldn't understand why we kept playing "Burnin and Lootin" by Bob Marley and the Wailers. I can still see his stupid good-looking face peering at me while he said: "But how can you listen to that type of material? They're singing about *you*. They want to burn and loot *you*."

The television audience was then treated to the sight of Ian, stoned out of his head on horse tranquillizer, smiling blissfully without even the politeness to act uncomfortable.

"We are," he said, "the Andy Warhols of business."

In the first six months, we had achieved almost 100 per cent distribution, increased sales by 228 per cent, introduced a new line of low-price dinners, and, as the seventh month finished, we began to look as if we might meet the profit forecast we had made.

We entertained the board of directors at a special luncheon. They were delighted with us.

10

The camp fires of the unemployed flicker around the perimeter. Tonight, once more, their numbers have increased. They grew from three, to six, to twenty. Now I choose not to count them. The unemployed have assumed the nature of a distinct and real threat. Yet they have done nothing. During grey days they have been nothing but poorly defined figures in a drab landscape, sitting, standing, concerned with matters I cannot imagine. They have done nothing to hamper trucks full of raw materials. Neither have they tried to intercept the freezer vans. Their inactivity sits most uneasily with their cancerous multiplication.

I can hear some of them singing. They sound like men on a bus coming home from a picnic.

The night buzzes with insects and great grey clouds roll across the sky, whipped across by a high, warm wind. Occasionally lightning flickers around the edge of the sky. Out in the scrub the mosquitoes must be fierce and relentless. It must be a poor feast for them.

Although the gate is guarded and the perimeter patrolled I have chosen to set up my own guard in this darkened window. It was not a popular decision. An open window makes the air-conditioning behave badly. Sergei thinks that I am being an alarmist but I have always been an alarmist.

I have spent my life in a state of constant fear that could be understood by very few. I have anticipated disaster at every turn, physical attack at every instant. To be born small and thin and poor, one learns, very quickly, of one's vulnerability. My fear kept me in constant readiness and it also gave me fuel for my most incredible defence. My strength has been my preparedness to do anything, to be totally crazy, to go past the limits that even the strongest will dare to contemplate. The extent of my terrible quaking fear was in exact correspondence with the degree of my craziness. For I performed unthinkable acts of cruelty to others, total bluffs that would prevent all thought of retaliation.

I learnt this early, as a child, when I got my nose busted up by a boy four years older and much, much bigger. I can still remember the bastard. He had wire-framed glasses and must have been blind in one eye because he had white tape obscuring one lens. I can remember the day after he bashed me. I can remember as if it were yesterday. I waited for him just around the side of the Catholic Church. There was a lane there which he always walked down and beside the lane was a big pile of house bricks, neatly stacked. I was eight years old. I waited for the bastard as he came down the lane kicking a small stone. He looked arrogant and self-confident and I knew I couldn't afford to fail. As he passed me I stood up and threw the first brick. It sounded soft and quiet as it hit his shoulder, but I'd thrown it so hard it knocked him over. He looked round with astonishment but I already had the second brick in the air. It gashed his arm. He started crying. His glasses had gone. They were on the ground. I stood on them. Then I kicked him for good measure.

The effectiveness of this action was greatly enhanced by the fact that I had been seen by others. It helped me get a reputation. I built on this with other bricks and great lumps of wood. I cut and burned and slashed. I pursued unthinkable actions with the fearful skill and sensitivity of someone who can't afford to have his bluff called. I developed the art of rages and found a way to let my eyes go slightly mad and, on occasions, to dribble a little. It was peculiar that these theatrical effects often became real. I forgot I was acting.

But there was no real defence against the fires of the unemployed. They were nothing more than threatening phantoms licking at the darkness. My mind drifted in and out of fantasies about them and indeed, inevitably, with the trap corridors of a maze, at the place where they killed or tortured me.

Below me Bart was sitting on the steps. I could hear him fiddling with his weapons. All week he has been working on a new, better, hand-tooled leather holster. Now it is finished he wears it everywhere. He looks good enough for the cover of *Rolling Stone*.

The unemployed are singing "Blowin' in the Wind". Burt starts to hum the tune along with them, then decides not to. I can hear him shifting around uncomfortably, but there is nothing I can say to him that would make his mind any more at ease.

The unemployed will have the benefit of their own holy rage.

It is difficult to see across the plant. The spotlights we rigged up seem to create more darkness than light. I stare into the darkness, imagining movements, and thinking about my day's work. Today I went through the last three months' cost reports and discovered that our raw material costs are up over 10 per cent on eight of our lines. This is making me edgy. Something nags at me about it. I feel irritable that no one has told me. But there is nothing that can be done until tomorrow.

The movement across the face of the No. 1 store is vague and uncertain. I rub my eyes and squint. Below me I can hear Bart shift. He has taken off his boots and now he moves out towards the No. 1, sleek as a night cat, his gun hand out from his side like a man in a movie. I hold my breath. He fades into almost-dark. The figure near the No. 1 stops and becomes invisible to me. At that moment there is a shot. The figure flows out of the dark, dropping quietly like a shadow to the ground.

I am running down the stairs, and am halfway across the apron before Bart has reached the No. 1. I pray to god he hasn't shot a guard.

"Not bad, eh? That's about fifty yards."

I don't say anything. He is fussing over his gun, replacing the dead shell with a live bullet. I let him walk ahead. I'm not going to get any fun out of this. He walks forward, as nonchalant as if he were going to change a record or go and get another drink.

I see his flashlight turn on and then a pause as he kneels to look at the body. And then the light goes out and he is running around and around in circles. He is yelping and running like a dog whose foot has been run over. As he circles he says, "Shit, Shit, Shit, oh fucking Christ." He looks comical and terrible dancing in his bare feet. He can't stay still. He runs around saying shit.

Then I am looking at the body. In the yellow light of my flashlight I see the face of a sixteen-year-old boy. I notice strange things, small details: golden down on the cheeks, bad pimples, and something else. At first, in dumb shock, I think it's his guts coming up. And a pea rolls out. In his mouth is a chunk of TV dinner, slowly thawing.

11

When I was six years old I threw a cat into an incinerator. It wasn't until the cat came running out the grate at the bottom, burning, screaming, that I had any comprehension of what I had done.

The burning cat still runs through my dreams searing me with its dreadful knowledge.

When I saw the dead boy I knew it was Bart's burning cat.

He is like the girls in *Vogue*, wearing combat clothes and carrying guns and smoking pink cigarettes. He is like the intellectuals: he lives on the wrong side of the chasm between ideas and action. The gap is exactly equal to the portion of time that separates the live cat from the burning cat.

That is the difference between us.

It should be said to him: "If you wear guns on your hip you will need to see young boys lying dead at your feet and confront what 'dead' is. That is what it takes to live that fantasy. If you cannot do this, you should take off your uniform. Others will perform the unpleasant acts for you. It is the nature of business that as a result of your decisions some people will starve and others be killed. It is simply a matter of confronting the effects of your actions. If you can grasp this nettle you will be strong. If you cannot, you are a fool and are deluding yourself."

12

Our burning cats are loose.

Bart's is sedated, slowed down, held tightly on a fearful leash by Mandies or some other downer. Perhaps he has been shooting up with morphine. His eyes are dull and his movements clumsy but his cat stirs threateningly within him, intimidating him with its most obvious horror.

My cat is loose and raging and my eyes are wide. Black smoke curls like friendly poison through my veins and bubbles of rage course through my brain. My cat is clawing and killing, victim and killer. I am in an ecstasy. I can't say. My eyes stretch wide and nostrils, also, are flaring.

Oh, the electricity. The batteries of torches firing little hits of electricity behind the eyes. To stretch my fingers and feel the tautness behind the knuckles like full sails under heavy wind.

For I have found out.

I have discovered a most simple thing. The little bastard Sergei has been cheating me in such a foolish and simple way that I cannot contain my rage at the insult to my intelligence. He has been siphoning funds like a punk. A dull stupid punk without inventiveness. He is someone trying to club a knife-fighter to death. He is so stupid I cannot believe it.

Ah, the rage. The rage, the fucking rage. He has no sense. He hasn't even the sense to be afraid. He stands before me, Bart by his side. Bart does not live here. He is away on soft beds of morphine which cannot ease his pain. Sergei is threatening. He is being smart. He thinks I'm a fool. He casts collusive glances towards Bart who is like a man lobotomized. Smiling vaguely, insulated by blankets of morphine from my rage, like a man in an asbestos suit in the middle of a terrible fire.

Oh, and fire it is.

For the cost of raw materials has not risen by 10 per cent. The cost of raw materials has not risen at all. Sergei, the fool, has been paying a fictitious company on his cheque butts and using the actual cheques to pay both the real suppliers and himself.

I only do this for the profit, for the safety, for the armour and strength that money gives. That I may be insulated from disaster and danger and threats and little bastards who are trying to subvert my friends and take my money.

And now there will be an example.

For he is trying to place me in a factory. He is trying to take my power. He shall be fucking well cut, and slashed, and shall not breathe to spread his hurt.

He is smart and self-contained. He speaks with the voice of the well-educated and powerful. His eyebrows meet across his forehead.

It took me three hours to trace his schoolboy fiddle. And it only took that long because the bastards who were doing the company's search took so long to confirm that the company he's been writing on his cheque butts doesn't exist. It took me five minutes to check that his prices were inflated. Five minutes to guess what he was up to.

The body of Bart's victim has been tied to the top of the perimeter fence. Let that warn the bastards. Even the wind will not keep down the flies. The unemployed shall buzz with power-less rage.

And now Sergei. An example will be made. I have called for his suit and his white business shirt and black shoes. The suit is being pressed. The shoes are being polished. It will be a most inventive execution, far more interesting than his dull childish cheating.

Under my surveillance his hair is being cut. Very neat. He is shaved cleanly. He is shaved twice. The poor idiot does not know what is happening. Bart watches with dumb incomprehension, helping the girl who is cutting the hair. He holds the bowl of hot water. He brings a towel. He points out a little bit of sideburn that needs trimming better. He is stumbling and dazed. Only I know. I have Bart's gun, just in case.

The suit is pressed. Bart helps with the tie. He fusses, tying and re-tying. Sergei's eyes have started to show fear. He tries to talk casually to me, to Bart. He is asking what is happening but Bart is so far away that his mind is totally filled with the simple problem of tying the tie, its loops and folds provide intricate problems of engineering and aesthetics.

I never liked Sergei. He never treated me with respect. He showed disdain.

I will donate him a briefcase. I have a beautiful one left me by the old general manager. It is slim and black with smart snappy little chrome clips on it. In it I place Sergei's excellent references and about five hundred dollars worth of cash. It is a shame about the money, but no one must ever think him poor or helpless.

I order him to hold the briefcase. He looks so dapper. Who could not believe he was a senior executive? Who indeed!

It is time now for the little procession to the gate. The knowledge of what is happening hits Sergei on this, his walk to the scaffold. He handles it well enough, saying nothing I remember.

High on the wire the dead boy stands like a casualty of an awkward levitation trick.

I have the main gate opened and Sergei walks out of it. The guards stand dumbly like horses in a paddock swishing flies away. I am watching Bart's eyes but they are clouded from me. He has become a foreign world veiled in mists. I know now that we will not discuss Dylan again or get stoned together. But he will do what I want because he knows I am crazy and cannot be deceived.

He seems to see nothing as the great wire mesh gate is rolled back into place and locked with chains. Sergei walks slowly down the gravel road away from us.

A grey figure slides out from the scrub a mile or so away. They will welcome him soon, this representative of management with his references in his briefcase.

The fact of Sergei's execution could not possibly be nearly as elegant as my plan. I return to my office, leaving the grisly reality of it to the watchers at the gate.

13

In the night they put Sergei's head on the wire. It stares towards my office in fear and horror, a reminder of my foolishness.

For now it appears that I misunderstood the situation. It appears that he was acting on Bart's instructions, that the siphoned funds were being used to rebuild the inside of the factory.

To please me, dear god.

How could I have guarded against Bart's "What if . . ." or protected us all from his laconic "easy-peasy"? If one lives with dreamers and encourages their aberrations something is bound to go wrong. Now I understand what it is to be the parent of brilliant children, children reared with no discipline, their every fantasy pandered to. Thus one creates one's own assassins.

The factory tour is over now and Bart sits in my office eyeing me with the cunning of a dog, pretending servility, but with confused plans and strategies showing in his dog-wet eyes.

He understood nothing of factories nor my fear of them. His model factory is a nightmare far more obscene that anything my simple mind could have creased.

For they have made a factory that is quiet. They have worried about aesthetics.

Areas of peaceful blue and whole fields of the most lyrical green. In these ideal conditions people perform insulting functions, successfully imitating the functions of mid-twentieth century machinery.

This is Bart and Sergei's masterpiece, their gift to me. They have the mentality of art students who think they can change the world by spraying their hair silver.

They make me think of other obscenities. For instance: a Georg Jensen guillotine made from the finest silver and shaped with due concern for function and aesthetic appeal. Alternatively: condemned cells decorated with pretty blue bunny patterns from children's nurseries.

In order to achieve these effects they have reduced profit by 6·5 per cent.

In here it is very quiet. No noise comes from the staff outside. I have seen them, huddled together in little groups at the windows staring at Sergei. They seem anaesthetized. They have the glazed eyes of people too frightened to see anything that might get them into trouble. Thus they avoided Bart's eyes. He pranced through like a spider, his hand on his gun, the fury in his veins bursting to fill the room like black ink in water.

Now in the silence of my office I see the extent to which he is afflicted by hurt and misunderstanding. Trying to talk to him, I put my hand on his arm. He flinches from me. In that terrible instant I am alone on the park ice, the string inside me taut and all that lonely ice going in front of me no matter which way I turn. And he, Bart, looking at me guilty and afraid and angry and does he want to kill me?

Yes, he does.

He will learn to use his burning cat. He hates me because I killed his friend. It was a misunderstanding. It was his fault, not mine. If they hadn't cheated I would never have made the mistake. His friend Sergei, the little turd, he thought he was clever but he was a fool. Sergei, his stupid mouth dribbling black blood on the top of the wire fence. If only his siphoning of funds had been more subtle. There were two other ways to do it, but he did it like a petty cash clerk. It was this which upset me the most. It was this which put me over the line and left me here, alone, threatened by the one person I thought my friend.

He may wish to kill me.

But I, alone on the ice, have eyes like the headlights of a truck. I have power. I will do anything. And I have made enough bad dreams that one more dying face will make not the slightest scrap of difference. Anyone who wants to cling on to their life won't fuck around with me too willingly, though their hand might easily encircle my wrist, though they have the strength to crush me with their bare arms, for I am fearful and my fear makes me mighty.

And I am not mad, but rather I have opened the door you all keep locked with frightened bolts and little prayers. I am more like you than you know. You have not inspected the halls and attics. You haven't got yourself grubby in the cellars. Instead you sit in the front room in worn blue jeans, reading about atrocities in the Sunday papers.

Now Bart will do as I wish for he wishes to live and is weak because of it. I am a freight train, black smoke curling back, thundering down the steel lines of terrible logic.

So now I speak to him so quietly that I am forcing him to strain towards me. Trucks have been destroyed attempting to enter the plant. It is time, I tell him, that the scrub be cleared of unemployed.

It will give him something to do. It will give him a use for his rage. He can think about his friend, whom I didn't kill. He was killed by the people in the scrub, whoever they are. They are the ones holding up trucks and stopping business, and business must go on. BUSINESS MUST GO ON. That is what the hell we are here for. There is no other reason for this. This is the time that is sold to the devil. It is time lost, never to be re-lived, time stolen so it can be OK later and I can live in white sheets and ironed shirts and drink gin and tonic in long glasses, well away from all this.

Then I can have the luxury of nightmares, and pay the price gladly, for it will only be my sleep which will be taken and not my waking hours as well.

14

All around the plant seemed very, very still. The sun had gone down, leaving behind a sky of the clearest blue I had ever seen. But even as I watched, this moment passed and darkness claimed it.

I watched Bart lead his contingent of workers through the dusk in the direction of the front gate. Each man had a flamethrower strapped to his back and I smiled to think that these men had been producing food to feed those whom they would now destroy.

I watched the operation from the roof of the canteen, using binoculars Sergei had left behind.

As I watched men run through the heat burning other men alive, I knew that thousands of men had stood on hills or roofs and watched such scenes of terrible destruction, the result of nothing more than their fear and their intelligence.

In the scrub the bodies of those who hated me were charred and smouldering.

I touched my arm, marvelling at the fineness of hairs and skin, the pretty pinkness glowing through the fingernails, the web-like mystery of the palm, the whiteness underneath the forearm and the curious sensitivity where the arm bends.

I wished I had been born a great painter. I would have worn fine clothes and celebrated the glories of man. I would have stood aloft, a judge, rather than wearily kept vigil on this hill, hunch-backed, crippled, one more guilty fool with blood on his hands.